'Falcon.'

Annie could hear the relief in her own voice as she half ran and half stumbled across the room, all but flinging herself into Falcon's arms, but she simply didn't care.

'They're trying to take him from me. They're trying to say that I'm a bad mother.'

'The child is a Leopardi,' she could hear the old Prince insisting. 'His place is here with—'

'With me.' Falcon stopped his father in mid-rant. 'And that is exactly where Oliver will be from now on. With me and with his mother, since she has agreed to be my wife. I shall be formally adopting him as my son.'

Falcon's arm was round her, supporting her, tightening in warning as she made a small, shocked sound of protest.

'And I should warn you that there is no law in this land or any other that will remove from me the right to be the guardian of my stepson, a child of my o———— ———— ——— protector of both him and hi————

THE LEOPARDI BROTHERS

Sicilian by name...
Scandalous, scorching and seductive by nature!

**Three darkly handsome Leopardi men believe
it is their duty to hunt down their missing heir—
as Sicilians, as sons, as brothers!**

**Falcon has found the child,
and he has found its mother...but he has also
discovered the dark secrets of his late half-brother.**

*'There is something I have to say to you,'
Falcon told Annie. 'Your right to your sexuality has
been stolen from you by a member of my sex, and the
damage that has been done has been compounded by a
member of my family. As a Leopardi, and the eldest of
my brothers, I have a duty to make recompense to you
and to restore to you what has been taken away. That
is the law of the Leopardi family,
and the code by which we live.'*

**In November look out for Penny Jordan's
new Modern™ Romance just in time for Christmas!**

THE SICILIAN'S BABY BARGAIN

BY
PENNY JORDAN

MILLS & BOON
Pure reading pleasure™

All the characters in this book have no existence outside the imagination of the author, and have no relation whatsoever to anyone bearing the same name or names. They are not even distantly inspired by any individual known or unknown to the author, and all the incidents are pure invention.

First published in Great Britain 2009
Harlequin Mills & Boon Limited,
Eton House, 18-24 Paradise Road, Richmond, Surrey TW9 1SR

© Penny Jordan 2009

ISBN: 978 0 263 87413 6

Set in Times Roman 10½ on 12¾ pt
01-0809-50641

Printed and bound in Spain
by Litografia Rosés, S.A., Barcelona

Penny Jordan has been writing for more than twenty years and has an outstanding record: over 170 novels published, including the phenomenally successful A PERFECT FAMILY, TO LOVE, HONOUR AND BETRAY, THE PERFECT SINNER and POWER PLAY, which hit the *Sunday Times* and *New York Times* bestseller lists. Penny Jordan was born in Preston, Lancashire, and now lives in rural Cheshire.

Recent titles by the same author:

THE SICILIAN BOSS'S MISTRESS
  (The Leopardi Brothers)
CAPTIVE AT THE SICILIAN BILLIONAIRE'S COMMAND
  (The Leopardi Brothers)
TAKEN BY THE SHEIKH
THE SHEIKH'S BLACKMAILED MISTRESS
VIRGIN FOR THE BILLIONAIRE'S TAKING

PROLOGUE

FALCON LEOPARDI grimaced in distaste. This was supposed to be a memorial gathering to mark what would have been the birthday of his late half-brother Antonio. It was their father's idea, and one that strictly speaking Falcon did not approve of—especially not an excuse to get drunk. But then the majority of Antonio's so-called friends obviously shared his late half-brother's love of over-indulgence just as they had shared his love of a louche lifestyle.

One of them was breathing alcoholic fumes over Falcon now, as he leaned drunkenly towards him confidingly and spoke to him.

'Did Tonio ever tell you about that woman whose drink he spiked in Cannes last year? He swore to us all that he'd get his revenge on her for turning him down, and he did that, all right. Last I heard she was trying to claim that he'd fathered the brat she was carrying.'

Falcon, who had been about to move away in disgusted irritation, turned back to look at the unpleasant specimen of manhood now reeling unsteadily in front of him.

'I seem to remember him mentioning something or other about the situation,' he lied. 'But why don't you refresh my memory?'

The drunk was more than happy to oblige.

'We'd seen her at Nikki Beach. She wasn't joining in the fun like the other girls there, even though she was with one of the film outfits. Always turned up in a blouse and skirt, looking like a schoolteacher. Antonio soaked the shirt with champagne for a joke, trying to get her to lighten up, but she wasn't having any of it. Really got his back up, she did—the way she treated him. Rejecting him like she was something special. He told us all he was going to have his revenge on her, and he certainly did that. He found out where she was staying, then he bribed one of the waiters to slip something into her drink. Knocked her out flat. It took three of us to get her back to her room. Of course Antonio swore us to secrecy, threatened us with a whole lot of bad stuff if what he'd done ever got out. 'Course, me telling you now is different, 'cos he's dead and you're his brother.' He hiccupped and then belched, before continuing. 'Tonio made us keep guard outside. He told us afterwards that she was so tight she must have been a virgin.'

The man's expression began to alter and his manner changed from one of swaggering confidence to something far more sheepish as Falcon's cold silence penetrated his drink-befuddled state, bringing home to him the true shameful reality of the horrific tale he was relating. 'Not that Tonio got away with it,' he rushed to reassure Falcon. 'He told me that her brother came after him, saying that he'd got her pregnant. But that there was no way he was going to do as she wanted and provide for the kid she was carrying.'

Falcon hadn't said a word whilst his late brother's friend had been speaking. He found it easy, though, to accept his late half-brother's role in the nasty, sordid little incident the other man had described to him. It was typical of

Antonio, and underlined—if any underlining had been necessary—exactly why Falcon and his two younger brothers had so disliked their half-brother during his short life and had not mourned his passing.

'What was her name? Can you remember?' he asked the drunk now.

The other man shook his head, and then frowned in concentration, before telling Falcon, 'Think it might have been Anna or Annie—something like that. She was English—I know that.'

As though Falcon's cold contempt chilled him, the drunk shivered and then staggered away. No doubt keen to find himself another drink, Falcon reflected as he looked across to where his two brothers and their wives were seated with his father.

Their father, the Prince, had worshipped and spoiled his youngest son, the only child he had had with the woman who had been his mistress during his marriage to the mother of his elder three sons' mother—his wife once she was dead.

He had claimed, after Antonio's death in a car accident, that Antonio's last words to him had been to say that he had a child—conceived whilst Antonio was in Cannes—and he had demanded that this child be found.

Falcon had believed that he had left no stone unturned trying to do this—without any success—but now realised that he had overlooked the fact that his brother had lived his life among the slimy waste of humanity that was expert at scuttling away from the too-bright light of overturned stones.

He knew what he had to do now, of course. The only question was whether or not he told his brothers before or after he found the woman his half-brother had drugged, raped and impregnated with his child—because find her he most certainly would. Even if he had to turn the whole world upside down to do so. His honour and his duty to the Leopardi name would accept nothing less. On balance, telling them first would be easier....

CHAPTER ONE

ANNIE rubbed her eyes. Well shaped and an intense shade of almost violet-blue, with thick long eyelashes, they were eyes any woman could be proud of—if they hadn't been aching with tiredness and feeling as though they were filled with grit. She lifted her hand, its wrist so slender that it looked dangerously fragile, pushing the heavy weight of her shoulder-length, naturally blonde and softly curling hair off her face. Normally she wore it scraped back in a neat knot, but Ollie had grabbed it earlier when she had been giving him his bath, and in the end it had been easier to leave it down. She loved her baby so much. He meant everything to her, and there was nothing she wouldn't do to protect him and keep him safe. Nothing.

She had been reading all evening. Part-time freelance research work didn't pay very well—certainly not as well as her previous job, which had been working as a researcher for a novelist turned playwright. Tom had paid her very well indeed, and he and his wife had become good friends. Annie's face clouded. The lighting in her small one-bedroom flat didn't really give off enough light for the demanding work she was doing—even if it was energy-efficient.

Next to her work on the cramped space of the small folding table there was a letter from her stepbrother amongst the post forwarded from her old address. She shivered and looked over her shoulder, almost as though she feared that Colin himself might suddenly materialise out of the ether.

Colin was living in the house that had originally belonged to her father, which should have been hers. He had stolen it from her—just as he had stolen… She flinched, not wanting to think about her stepbrother.

But there were times when she had to do so, for Ollie's safety. Her stepbrother disapproved of the fact that she had kept Ollie, instead of having him put up for adoption as he had wanted her to do. But nothing could make her willingly part with her baby—not even Colin's attempts to make her feel guilty for keeping him. He had insisted, that someone else—a couple—would give him a better life than she could as a single mother. Colin could be very convincing and persuasive when he wanted to be. She had been desperately afraid that he would win others over to his cause.

Sometimes she felt that she would never be able to stop looking over her shoulder, afraid that Colin had tracked them down and that somehow he would succeed in parting her from her son.

She would never even have told him about her pregnancy, but Susie, the wife of the author she had been working for when 'it'—her rape by Antonio Leopardi—had happened, had thought she was doing her a favour by writing to him and telling him what had happened. Susie had been thrilled when Colin had offered her a home after Ollie's birth, and all the support she needed.

Annie had refused his offer, though. She, after all, knew him far better than Susie did. Instead she had stayed in her flat, using the excuse that she wanted Ollie to be born at the local hospital because of its excellent reputation.

Colin had refused to be put off and had insisted on continuing to visit her. Initially he had even pretended that he agreed with her decision to keep her baby once it was born, but that pretence had soon vanished once he'd realised that Antonio Leopardi was not going to respond to Colin's demand for financial support for his son.

Not that Colin had said anything of this to Susie and Tom, who had been so kind to her.

In the end Annie had begun to feel so desperate and so pressured, afraid that somehow Colin might succeed in forcing her and her baby apart, that a few weeks after Ollie's birth, whilst Colin had been away in Scotland, sorting out the affairs of an elderly cousin of his father's who had recently died, she had decided not to renew the lease on her existing flat and to move away instead, to start a new life for herself and Ollie.

Without telling anyone what she was doing—not even Susie and Tom, who had so obviously been taken in by Colin—she had found herself a new flat and new work, and then she had simply disappeared, leaving strict instructions that her forwarding address must remain confidential. It had been easy enough to do in a big city like London.

That had been five months ago now. But she still didn't feel safe—not one little bit.

She had felt guilty not saying anything to Susie and Tom, but she couldn't afford to take any risks. They didn't know Colin as she did, and they didn't know what he was capable of doing—or how intensely single-minded he could be. She shivered again, remembering how unhappy she had been when their parents had first married, and how she had tried to explain to her mother how apprehensive and ill at ease Colin had made her feel, with his concentrated focus on her, watching everything she did.

He had been away at university then, aged nineteen to her twelve, but after their parents had married—he had decided to change courses, and had ended up living at home and travelling daily to his new university.

Colin had taken a dislike to her best friend Claire, and Annie's mother had suggested to Annie that it might be better if Claire didn't come to the house any more after an incident during which Colin had nearly reversed his father's car into Claire whilst she had been riding her bike.

And now Colin had taken a dislike to Ollie. Annie shivered again.

She had never known her own father. A soldier, from a long line of army men, he had died in an ambush abroad before she had been born. But Annie had been very happy growing up with her mother.

Her father had left them very well provided for—there had been money in his family which had come down to him, and Annie's mother had always told Annie it would ultimately come down to her. But now it was Colin's, because her mother had died before her second husband, meaning that the house had passed into his hands and then into Colin's. The home that should have been hers and Oliver's was denied to them.

Automatically she looked anxiously towards her son's cot. Ollie was fast asleep. Unable to resist the temptation, she got up and went to stand looking down at him. He was so beautiful, so perfect, that sometimes just looking at him filled her with so much awe and love that she felt as though her heart would burst with the pressure of it. He was a good baby, healthy and happy, and so gorgeous—with his head of silky dark curls and his startling blue-grey eyes with thick black lashes—that people constantly stopped to admire him. He was bright too, and full of curiosity about the world around him.

They adored him at the council-run nursery where she had to leave him every weekday whilst she went off to her cleaning job—the only other work she had been able to get without too many questions being asked. Most of the others on the team of agency cleaners she worked with were foreign—hard working, but reluctant to talk very much about themselves.

Her present life was a world away from the world in which she had grown up and the future she had expected to have. Ollie's childhood, unlike hers, would not be spent in a large comfortable house with its own big garden on the edge of a picturesque Dorset village. The area of the city where they lived was run-down, with large blocks of flats—once she would have been horrified at the thought of living here, but now she welcomed its anonymity and its fellow inhabitants, who neither welcomed questions nor asked them.

Ollie opened his eyes and looked up at her, giving her a beaming smile. Annie felt her insides melt. She loved him so much. What an extraordinary thing mother love was— empowering her to love her son despite the horror of his conception.

She flinched again. She tried never to think about what had happened to her in Cannes. Mercifully she had no memory of her ordeal, thanks to the drug that had been slipped into her drink. Susie, who had found her in her room, still drugged and dazed late in the morning after the night of the rape, had wanted her to go to the police but she had refused—too much in shock and too fearful to trust them to believe her. Susie had been wonderfully kind to her. Annie missed her kindness and her friendship.

Like Colin, Susie had felt that her rapist should be forced at least to financially support his child, and it had been Susie who had supplied her stepbrother with Antonio's name—something Annie herself had refused to do.

Annie hadn't been surprised when Antonio had refused to do anything, and she had felt relieved when she had read in the papers about Antonio's death. Now there would never be any need for Ollie to have to learn about his father or how he had been conceived. Unless Colin found them.

Her stomach clenched. He couldn't. He mustn't. And she mustn't think about him doing so just in case somehow her thoughts enabled it to happen.

She thought of herself as a logical, realistic sort of person, well aware of the harsh reality of life, but sometimes at times like this, when she felt so dreadfully alone, she wished that there were such a thing as fairy godmothers who, with one wave of a magical wand, could somehow transport her and Ollie to a place where they could be together and safe, where Colin simply couldn't reach them.

If she believed in fairy godmothers, guardian angels and wishes then that would be her wish—but of course she didn't. And wishes couldn't come true just because one wished them.

The foyer of the five-star hotel was empty of any of its wealthy guests as Annie got down on her hands and knees to remove a piece of trodden-down chewing gum from the marble floor. Her shift was actually over, but the receptionist—who seemed to have taken a dislike to her—had insisted that she pick up the litter dropped, Annie was sure quite deliberately, by the woman who had walked through the lobby a few minutes earlier. Her high heels had clacked on the marble floor, and her look of contempt for Annie had been all too plain as she'd smoothed down the skirt of her no-doubt expensive outfit and then dropped the chewing gum on the floor.

The sun was shining outside, its brilliant rays getting in Annie's eyes and dazzling her. She blinked, raising her head in an attempt to avoid the too-bright light.

Falcon wasn't in a very good mood. He had flown into London earlier in the week and had gone straight to a meeting with the head of what was supposed to be the country's best missing person tracking agency, only to be told that whilst the agency had initially managed to identify Annie Johnson as the mother of Antonio's child, she had disappeared five months ago, taking her baby with her, and they had not as yet managed to find her.

Falcon had spent a fruitless afternoon with Annie's stepbrother, to whom he had taken an instant dislike, and now he had received a message from his youngest brother Rocco, telling him that their father's health had suffered a sudden decline.

'He's stable now, and back at the *castello.*' Rocco had told him. 'But the hospital says that he is very frail.'

He needed to be in Sicily, Falcon knew, he had a duty to his family to be there. But he also had a duty to this child conceived so casually by his half-brother, and denied by him as though he was no more than a piece of detritus. Falcon had never liked Antonio. He hadn't thought it was possible for his contempt for him to increase, but he had been wrong.

As he stepped into the foyer of his hotel, his eyes shielded from the glare of the sun by gold-rimmed discreetly non-logoed Cartier glasses, the first thing he saw was a cleaner, kneeling on the floor beside her bucket of dirty water. She was wearing a body-shrouding, washed-out blue overall and her hair was scraped back from her make-up-free face, but when she lifted her face to avoid the sunlight glaring into her eyes, Falcon's heart turned over inside his chest and his heart started to race.

It was her. There was no mistake. After all, he'd only just left the office where her photograph had been pinned to the file in front of him. There was no mistaking those intensely blue eyes, nor that elegantly boned and beautifully structured face, with its small straight nose and its softly full mouth—even if right now her skin was drained of life and her expression etched in lines of exhaustion.

The hand she'd reached out to remove the flat grey-white pat of chewing gum that someone had left on the otherwise immaculate floor was red and swollen, her wrist thin and fragile, and her scraped back hair was out of sight beneath some sort of protective cover. But it was her. By some miracle, it was her.

The receptionist was still glowering at her, causing Annie to feel a sudden rush of anger. She had worked over her allotted hours, time for which she would not be paid, and the chewing gum wasn't her responsibility. She stood up abruptly—and then gasped as her action brought her into immediate physical contact with someone. Not just some-one, she recognised as male hands came out to grab her, somehow sliding up under the gaping arms of her overall to fasten round her bare skin. His intention was to fend her off, she imagined, rather than save her from stumbling, since such a man was hardly likely to care about the fate of someone like her. He was wearing an expensive suit, his eyes shielded from her inspection by dark-lensed sun-glasses, and his hair were dark and his skin tanned.

He was still holding her—waiting for her to apologise for daring to breathe the same air as him, she thought bitterly. She tugged away from him, only to have his grip on her arms tighten. She looked up at him. A discomfort-ing feeling was running through her body, its source the point of contact between his hands and her skin. Her pulse had started to jump and she was breathing too fast as her heart raced. She felt dizzy, her lungs starved of oxygen as though she had forgotten how to breathe and yet she *was* breathing—although very unsteadily.

Sensations like the mechanics of a long-unused piece of machinery were coming to painful life inside her. She wanted, she discovered in bemused disbelief, to lean into him, to have his arms come fully around her so that she was held against his maleness. A shudder ripped through her, and her body was hot with guilt and shame.

The most extraordinary feeling had Falcon in its grip. He didn't know what it was or where it had come from. The only comparison that came readily to his mind was a mem-ory of being young and standing on the edge of one of Sicily's most dangerous clifftops in the middle of a fierce storm, feeling the wind buffet him, knowing that it could take him and do what it wished with him. He had both wanted to fight its power and give in to it. What he'd felt was a mixture of awe and exhilaration, an awareness of a great power and a desire to test himself against it. It was a sense of being alive, heightened and stretched taut, of being on the edge of something dangerous and compelling.

The receptionist had left her desk and was coming towards them. Somehow Annie managed to wrench herself free and pick up her bucket so that she could make a speedy exit. She could hear the receptionist apologising as she did so.

CHAPTER TWO

SACKED. She had been sacked because a hotel guest had—shock, horror—had to *touch* her. The hotel receptionist had obviously reported the incident, and a complaint had then been made to the firm that employed her. Her manager had been waiting for her when she had returned with the other workers to the depot, to give her the news. As a part timer she had no comeback. She was now out of a job.

It was supposed to be summer, but the morning's bright sunshine had now gone and it had started to rain. As she stepped out into the street Annie hunched into her raincoat—a good-quality trenchcoat that belonged to her previous life, a life before the death of her mother and the birth of her son.

She was twenty-four years old, she reminded herself. Far too old to cry because she was alone and vulnerable and desperately worried about how she was going to hold everything together without her cleaning job.

The city streets were busy now, and she didn't want to be late collecting Ollie from his nursery. There'd been a notice pinned up in the nursery asking for teachers' assistants at the nearby primary school. Annie would have loved to have applied, but it was too dangerous. They'd check up on her and discover that Antonio's clever lawyers had threatened to sue her for claiming that he'd raped her, saying that in reality she had consented to having sex with him. Her reputation would be ruined. She had no proof that she had been raped. It had been her word against his and she couldn't even remember what had happened. She knew beyond any shadow of a doubt, though, that she would not have consented.

Her stepbrother had been furious when he had received that telephone call from Antonio's solicitors. He had been so sure that Antonio would pay up. She shivered, even though it wasn't cold, and then pinned a forced smile to her face as she climbed the short flight of stone steps that led to the door of the nursery.

The sunny yellow-painted hall walls were decorated with the children's brightly coloured artwork, and Mrs Nkobu, one of the more senior staff, greeted her with a warm smile.

'There's a man waiting to see you. Mrs Ward wasn't for letting him—she told him it was against the rules—but it's plain to see that he's the kind that doesn't pay attention to anyone's rules but his own,' she told Annie conspiratorially.

Fear iced down Annie's spine.

Colin had found them.

Strictly speaking the nursery wasn't supposed to allow anyone not authorised by a parent to have access to any of the children, but Annie knew how persuasive Colin could be. Nausea curdled her stomach. He would try to take over her life again. He would say it was in her best interests. He would remind her that their parents had left their assets to him because they trusted him to look after her—even though her mother had told her that the house would come to her, because it had belonged to her father.

She mustn't think about any of that now, she told herself. She would need all her energy and strength to survive the present; she mustn't waste it on the past.

'He's in the carers' room,' Mrs Nkobu informed her, referring to the small fusty room with a glass wall through which parents and guardians could watch the children whilst waiting to collect them.

Annie nodded her head, but instead of going to the carers' room she went to the nursery, busy with other mothers collecting their children. Ollie was sitting on the floor, playing with some toys, and as always when she saw him Annie's heart flooded with love. The minute he saw her he held out his arms to her to be picked up. Only once she was cradling him tightly in her arms did she feel brave enough to look through the glass panels into the room beyond them.

There was only one person there. He was standing with his back to the glass and he was not Colin. But any relief she might have felt was obliterated by the shock of recognition that arced through her, sending through her exactly the same tingling sensation of deadened sensory nerve-endings awakened into painful life as she had felt earlier in the hotel lobby, when he had held her.

A long-ago memory of herself as a young teenager came back to her. Inside her head she could see herself, giggling with a schoolfriend over a handsome young teenage pop idol they had both had a crush on. She had felt so alive then—so happy, and so unquestioningly secure in her unfolding sexuality. She held Ollie even tighter, causing him to wriggle in her arms at the same moment as the man from the hotel lobby turned round.

He wasn't wearing his sunglasses now, and she could see his eyes.

The breath left her lungs with so much force that it might as well have been driven out by a physical blow. She knew who or rather *what* he was immediately. How could she not when the eyes set in the scimitar-harsh maleness of his face were her son's eyes? That he and Ollie shared the same blood was undeniable—and yet he looked nothing like Ollie's father, the man who had raped her. Antonio Leopardi had had a soft, full-fleshed face, and pebble-hard brown eyes set too close together. He had been only of medium height, and thickset. This man was tall with broad shoulders, and his body—as she already knew—was hard with muscles, not soft with over-indulgence. He smelled of clean skin, and some cologne so subtle she couldn't put a name to it, not of alcohol and heavy after-shave.

He was clean-shaven, his thick dark hair groomed, whereas Antonio had favoured stubble and his hair thickly gelled.

Everything about this man said that he set the highest of standards for himself even more than for others. This man's word, once given, would be given for all time.

Everything about Antonio had said that he was not to be trusted, but despite their differences this man had to be related to her abuser. Ollie was the proof of that.

She wanted to turn and run, fear tumbling through her as she felt her defences as weak as a house of cards; but her fear was not fear of the man because he was a man, Annie had time to recognize. It was a different fear from the one that lay inside her like a heavy stone. Instinctively she knew that this man was no threat to *her*, and that *she* was in no danger from him. His focus wasn't on her. It was on her son—on Ollie.

Her mouth had gone dry and her heart was pounding recklessly, using up her strength. There was no escape for her. She knew that. Still she tried to delay the inevitable, her hands trembling as she strapped Ollie into his buggy and then reluctantly pushed it to the door.

He was waiting for her in the corridor, one strong, lean brown hand reaching for the buggy, forcing her to move her own hand or risk having him close his hand over her own.

Falcon frowned as he registered her reaction to him. Was her recoil part of the legacy Antonio had left her? He had been struck when he had seen her earlier by her vulnerability, and by his unfamiliar desire to reassure her. Now that feeling had returned.

Falcon wasn't used to experiencing such strong feelings for anyone outside his immediate family. He had never denied to himself his protective love for his two younger brothers, nor his belief that, as their elder, in the absence of their father's love and their mother's presence in their lives, it was his responsibility to protect and nurture them.

He had grown up shouldering that responsibility, but he had never before felt that fierce tug of emotional protectiveness towards anyone else.

It was because of the child, of course. There could be no other reason for his illogical reaction.

It had taken him several hours of impatient telephone calls and pressure to track her down via the agency that had employed her—thanks to that wretched receptionist preventing him from following her at the hotel.

This morning he had felt sorry for her. Now he was motivated solely by his duty to his family name to make amends for what Antonio had done, he assured himself.

And of course to ensure that Antonio's son grew up knowing his Leopardi heritage. It had taken him longer than he
had wished and a great deal of money to track him down,
but now that he had there could be no doubting that the
child was a Leopardi. He had known that the minute he had
seen him at the nursery. The boy's blood was stamped into
his features, and Falcon had seen from the woman's expression when she had looked at him that she knew that
too.

They were outside now, with no one to overhear them.

'Who are you?' Annie demanded unsteadily. 'And what
do you want?'

'I am Falcon Leopardi, the eldest of Antonio's half-
brothers from our father's first marriage.'

Colin had mentioned Antonio's family to her—or rather
he had tried to. But she had refused to listen. Antonio had,
after all, refused to acknowledge his son.

'You are Antonio's *brother*?'

The tone of her voice betrayed disbelief, and Falcon de-
tected a deeper core of something that sounded like revulsion. He could hardly blame her for that. In fact, he shared
her revulsion.

'No,' he corrected her grimly. 'We were only half-
brothers.'

How well she understood that need to differentiate and
distance oneself from a supposed sibling. But how ridiculous of her to allow herself to imagine that she and this man
could have anything in common, could share that deep-
rooted antipathy and guilt that had been so much a part of
her growing up.

Even now she could still her mother saying plaintively,
almost pleadingly, 'But, darling, Colin is just trying to be

friends with you. Why can't you be nicer to him?' She had tried so hard to tell her mother how she had felt, but how could you explain what you did not understand yourself? In the end it had driven a wedge between them—a gulf on one side of which stood Colin, the good stepchild, and on the other side her, the bad daughter.

Where had she gone? Falcon wondered, watching the shadows seeping pain as they darkened her eyes. Wherever it was it was somewhere in her past, he recognized. The quality of her silence held a message of her helpless inability to change anything.

It was the present and the future that he was here for, though.

She must resent Antonio—more than resent him, he would have thought. Although her love for her child was obvious, and backed up by all the information his enquiry agents had been able to gather. She was an exemplary and devotedly loving mother. Apart from the fact that for some reason she had turned down her stepbrother's offer of a home under his roof. Colin Riley had not been able to furnish him with a logical explanation for that, although he *had* implied that there had been some kind of quarrel which she, despite all his attempts to repair the damage, had refused to make up.

'She's always been inclined to be over-emotional and to overreact,' he had told Falcon. 'All I wanted to do—all I've *ever* wanted to do—is help her.'

'There was no love lost between the three of us and Antonio.'

Falcon's voice, his English perfect and unaccented, brought Annie back out of the past.

'I will not seek to hide that fact from you—nor the fact

that Antonio was our father's favourite son. I can also assure you that Antonio's choice of lifestyle was not ours. It could never have been and was never condoned by us.'

Annie looked at him, and then looked away again, her heart jumping as it always did whenever she had to think about Ollie's conception. Falcon Leopardi was obviously trying to tell her that he and his brothers were not tarred with the same brush as their younger half-brother. His choice of the word *'assure'* suggested that convincing her that his morals were very different from his half-brother was something he was determined to do. But why?'

'As to what I want…'

He paused for so long that Annie looked at him again, hard fingers of uncertainty and unease tightening round her heart when she saw that he was looking at Ollie.

'Before his death,' Falcon continued, 'Antonio told our father that there was a child. But he died before he could give more details. Such was the love our father felt for Antonio that he demanded that this child be traced. When no child could be found we assumed that laying claim to its existence had been another example of Antonio's enjoyment of deceit.'

Falcon paused again. She'd kept her gazed fixed straight ahead of her whilst he was speaking, but he could see from the way her grip had tightened on the buggy how tense she was.

The tale of what had been done to her was one of breathtakingly callous cruelty that would fill any decent person with revulsion. The only merciful aspect of it was that she herself apparently had no recollection of what had occurred. There was no doubt in Falcon's mind that the rape had been a deliberate act of punishment, intended to humiliate her—not conducted because Antonio had hoped to arouse her to passion and desire for him. That fitted in so well with everything Falcon knew about his half-brother's warped personality.

'Naturally, when it came to my knowledge that there might after all be a child, I had to find out the truth.'

He had stopped walking now, forcing Annie to do the same.

'How…how did it come to your knowledge?' She had to force the words out.

Falcon looked at her. He believed strongly in telling the truth. The truth, after all, was the only worthwhile foundation for anything that was worth having.

'A friend of Antonio's told me about your drink being spiked, about what he did, and I put two and two together.'

Annie had a childish desire to close her eyes, as though somehow by shutting everything out she could magically make herself disappear. Just to hear him say those words was as searingly humiliating as though she had been stripped naked in the street. Worse, because they ripped away her protection, laying bare her private shame.

'I know you contacted Antonio to tell him of the birth of his son—'

'No.' Annie checked him immediately, her pride reasserting itself. 'I didn't contact him. I would never— It was my stepbrother who did that. I didn't know about it until…until Colin told me that Antonio was denying that— that anything had happened.'

Falcon frowned. Was this perhaps the cause of the quarrel between them?

'Your stepbrother didn't mention anything about Antonio denying he had fathered your child when I spoke to him. He was most concerned about you, and asked me to keep him informed of any progress I might make in my search for you.'

Annie felt as though her heart had stopped beating.

She turned towards Falcon, imploring him. 'You haven't…you haven't told him where I am, have you?'

Falcon's frown deepened.

'He told me that his sole aim is to help and protect you.'

To help and protect *her*, but not Ollie. Colin didn't want anything to do with her baby, and if he had his way, Ollie would be removed from her life for ever.

How long did she have before Colin found her and started waging his relentless war to make her have Ollie adopted all over again? Panic clawed at her stomach. Everyone had always said how lucky she was to have such a devoted stepbrother, but they didn't know him as she did.

'He mustn't know where we are.'

In her panic she had revealed more than was wise, Annie recognised as she saw the way Falcon Leopardi was watching her. He was waiting for her to elaborate, to give him a logical reason as to why she didn't want Colin to find them.

'Colin believes that it would be better if Ollie was adopted,' she eventually managed to tell him.

Because he had not been able to get Antonio to pay up? Or because he felt it was the best option for the child? Falcon didn't think he needed to spend much time considering the two options. Colin had asked him specifically if there were any assets likely to come to Oliver from Antonio's estate or his family.

'But you don't agree with him?' Falcon asked now.

'No. I could never give him up. *Never*. Nothing and no one could ever make me do so.'

The passion in her expression and her voice changed her completely, bringing her suddenly to life, revealing the true perfection of her delicate beauty.

Falcon felt as though someone had suddenly punched him in the chest, rendering him unable to get his breath properly.

'I agree that a child as young as Oliver needs his mother,' he told her, as soon as he was back in control of himself. 'However, your son is a Leopardi—and as such it is only right and proper that he grows up amongst his own family and his own people in his own country. It is my duty to Oliver and to my family to ensure that he is raised as a Leopardi—and that you, as his mother, are treated as the mother of a Leopardi should be treated. That is why I am here. To take you both back to Sicily with me.'

Annie stared at him. His talk of duty was a world apart from the world she knew. Such a word belonged to another time, a feudal ancient time, and yet somehow it resonated within her.

'You want to take Ollie and me to Sicily—to live there?' she asked unsteadily, spacing out the words to clarify them inside her own head and make sure she had not misunderstood him.

His 'yes' was terse—like the brief inclination of his head.

'But you have no proof that Ollie is—'

The look he was giving her caused her to go silent.

'The evidence of his blood is quite plain to both of us,' he told her. 'You have seen it yourself.' He paused and looked down at the stroller before looking back to her. 'The child could be mine. He bears the Leopardi stamp quite clearly.'

His! Why did that assertion strike so compellingly into her heart?

'He doesn't look anything like Antonio.' He was all she could manage to say.

'No,' Falcon agreed. 'Antonio took after his mother, which I dare say is why our father loved him so much. He was obsessed by her, and that obsession killed our own mother and destroyed our childhood, depriving us of our father's love and our mother's presence. That will not happen to your child. In Sicily he will have you—his mother—the love and protection of his uncles, and the companionship of his cousins. He will be a Leopardi.'

He made it all sound so simple and so…so right. But she knew nothing of him of or his family other than that he had taken the trouble to track them down because he wanted Ollie.

How could she trust him—a stranger?

As though Falcon sensed her anxiety, he asked, 'You love your son, don't you?'

'Of course I do.'

'Then you must surely want what is best for him?'

'Yes,' Annie agreed helplessly.

'You will agree, I think, that he will have a far better life growing up in Sicily as a Leopardi than he could have here?'

'With a mother who works as a cleaner, you mean?' Annie challenged him.

'I am not the one who makes the rules of economics that say a financially disadvantaged child will suffer a great deal of hardship in his life. And besides, it is not just a matter of money—although of course that is important. You are alone in the world—you no longer have any contact with your stepbrother; you are all the family Oliver has. That is not healthy for a child, and it has been proven that is especially not healthy for a boy child to have only his mother. In Sicily, Oliver will have a proper family. If you love him as much as you claim, then for his sake you will be willing to come to Sicily. What, after all, is there to keep you here?'

If his last question was brutal it was also truthful, Annie admitted. There was *nothing* to keep her here—except of course that you did not go off to a foreign country with a man you did not know. You especially did not do so when you had a six-month-old beloved child to protect.

But in Sicily there would no Colin to fear. No dread of waking up to find her stepbrother leaning over Oliver's cot with that fixed look on his face, as she had once found him when he had visited her shortly after Ollie's birth.

Something—she didn't know what, other than that it was some deep core instinct—told her that in Falcon Leopardi's hands her precious son would be safe, and that those hands would hold him surely and protectively against all danger.

But what about her? What about the disquieting, unwanted, dangerous reaction she sensed within herself to him as a woman to his man? Panic seized her but she fought it down. It was Ollie she had to think of now, not herself. His needs and not hers. Falcon Leopardi was right to say that Ollie would have a far better life in Sicily as a Leopardi than he ever could here in London alone with her. When she added into that existing equation the potential threat of her stepbrother there was only one decision she could take, wasn't there?

As she struggled to come to terms with what the surrender of herself and her son into Falcon's care would mean, she reminded herself that only this morning she had laughed at herself for wishing for the impossible—for the magical waving of a wand to transport her somewhere she and Ollie could be safe.

That impossible had now happened, and she must, *must* seize the opportunity—for her son's sake. For Ollie. Nothing mattered more to her than her baby.

A strange dizzying sensation had filled her, making her feel giddy and weightless, as though she might almost float above the pavement. It took her several seconds to recognise that the feeling was one of relief at the removal of a heavy weight.

People would think she was crazy, going off with a man she didn't know, trusting her son to him. If she confided in Susie and Tom, who had been so kind in drumming up research work for her among Tom's writing friends while she was pregnant, they would ask questions and warn her to be careful. Susie would remind her of Colin's offer and look reproachfully at her. Susie had never understood why she hadn't accepted Colin's offer of a home. She had thought him kind and concerned. She had agreed with him about the benefits of having Ollie adopted.

How desperately she regretted letting slip to Susie in a moment of weakness that she had a stepbrother, and then letting Susie coax his name and address out of her. Susie had meant well when she had contacted him behind her back, believing that she was doing the right thing, and Colin had behaved in an exemplary fashion—playing the role of caring stepbrother to the hilt during her pregnancy, taking charge of everything.

'What happens if I refuse?' Annie asked now.

Falcon had been expecting her question.

'If you refuse, then I shall pursue my rights as Oliver's blood relative through the courts.'

He meant it, Annie recognised.

'You're asking me to accept a great deal on trust,' she pointed out. 'I have no reason to trust your family and every reason not to do so.'

'Antonio was never a true Leopardi. By his behaviour he dishonoured himself and our name, just as he dishonoured you. It is my duty to put right that wrong. You have my word that you will come to no harm whilst you are under my protection—from anyone or anything.'

Feudal words to match his feudal mindset, Annie thought, more affected by what he had said than she wanted to admit. He was offering her something she already knew she craved: respite and safety. What option did she have other than to take them when they were offered?

She sucked in a steadying breath, and then asked as calmly as she could, 'When would we have to leave?'

She had given in far more easily than Falcon had expected. Was that a reason for him to feel suspicious of her? Suspicious? No. After all, he knew all there was to know about her. But curious? Perhaps, yes.

'Soon,' he answered her. 'The sooner the better. My father isn't well. In fact, he is very frail, and it is his greatest wish to see Antonio's child.'

'There are things I shall need to do,' Annie began.

The reality of what she had committed to—not just herself but more importantly Oliver too—was only just beginning to sink in. But she could tell from Falcon Leopardi's expression that he would not allow her to have any second thoughts.

'Such as?' he questioned, confirming her thoughts.

'I shall have to notify Ollie's nursery—and the council. And I'll need to check to see if Ollie needs any special injections for Sicily.'

'He doesn't. And as for the nursery and your flat, you can safely leave all that to me. You will, however, both need clothes suitable for a hot climate. It is high summer in Sicily now.'

New clothes? How on earth was she going to afford those?

Humiliatingly, as though he had guessed what she was thinking, Falcon continued smoothly, 'Naturally I shall cover the cost of whatever is needed.'

'We aren't charity cases.' Humiliation made Annie snap. 'I'm not letting you buy our clothes.'

'No? Then I shall have to telephone ahead to one of my sisters-in-law and ask them to provide a suitable wardrobe for you both. They are both English, by the way, so I expect you will find you have a great deal in common with them. My youngest brother Rocco and his wife already have one adopted child—a boy the same age as Oliver.'

His brothers had English wives? She would have other female company? A little of Annie's anxiety receded—only to return as she wondered how his brothers' wives would react to her.

'Do you all live together?' she asked uncertainly. She had only the haziest knowledge of Italian family life—and none at all of aristocratic Sicilian family life.

'Yes and no. Rocco has his own home on the island, whilst Alessandro and I both have our own apartments within the Leopardi *castello*, where my father also lives. A suite of rooms will be made ready for your occupation.'

'Mine and Ollie's?' Annie checked.

'Of course. His place is with you. I have already said so. Now—' Falcon flicked back his cuff to look at his watch '—we shall meet tomorrow morning in order to do necessary shopping. I shall call for you both at your flat and then with any luck we should be ready to leave for Sicily tomorrow evening. I shall request Alessandro to have a private jet made ready for us. As for all the necessary paperwork with regard to your life here, as I said, you may safely leave all of that to me.'

'And you won't tell Colin that you've found me?'

She hadn't meant to ask, and she certainly hadn't meant to sound so pathetically and desperately in need of reassurance, but it was too late to wish the plea unspoken now. Falcon was looking at her, searching her face as though seeking confirmation of something? Of what? Her fear of Colin?

'No, I won't tell him,' Falcon confirmed. She was afraid of her stepbrother. He had guessed it already, but her reaction now had confirmed his suspicion. But why?

'If he finds me, he'll only try to persuade me to give Ollie up for adoption.' Annie felt obliged to defend her plea.

Falcon nodded his head and repeated, 'I won't tell him.'

It was well into the early hours when Annie woke abruptly out of an uneasy sleep, her heart thudding too fast and her senses alert, probing the darkness of the unlit room for the source of the danger that had infiltrated her sleep. Outside in the London street beyond the flat a motorbike backfired, bringing a juddering physical relief to her tensed nerve endings.

She looked towards the cot where Ollie lay sleeping,

and prayed that she had done the right thing in agreeing to go to Sicily—that she hadn't exchanged one form of imprisonment for another. As long as Ollie was safe that was all that mattered. Nothing else. *Nothing*.

CHAPTER THREE

TRUE to his word, Falcon Leopardi had arrived at the flat early in the morning to collect her and Ollie in the chauffeur-driven car he had hired. He had taken them to Harvey Nichols, where they had spent over an hour and more money than Annie liked to think about equipping Ollie with suitable clothes and a large amount of baby equipment for his new life.

Now, surveying what looked like a positive mountain of small garments, Annie felt guilty. She had been enjoying herself so much, choosing everything for him.

'I'm sorry.' She apologised to Falcon. 'I've chosen far too much, and it's all so expensive. Perhaps we should think again?'

'I shall be the judge of what is and is not expensive—and we don't have time for second thoughts. You still have your own wardrobe to attend to—although, I imagine that is something you can do far more comfortably without my presence.'

He pushed back the cuff of his suit jacket—a habit of his, Annie had noticed. In a different suit this morning, in a light tan that looked very continental, he had had all the super-thin and super-pretty salesgirls turning their heads to look at him.

'I've booked a personal shopper for you, so I'll leave you to it and come back in an hour.'

Annie nodded her head. He was leaving her to her own devices because he had other things to do—not because somehow or other he had known how on edge the thought of him standing over her whilst she selected hot weather clothes had made her. She mustn't start elevating him to the status of something approaching a mind-reading saint. But she did feel more comfortable knowing that he wouldn't be standing there, silently assessing her choices, ready to point out all the reasons why it wasn't suitable.

As a little girl she had loved pretty clothes and going shopping with her mother, just the two of them, but all that had changed once her mother had remarried. Colin had complained that she wasn't giving their new extended family a chance to work when she told her mother that she didn't like shopping with her stepfather and Colin in tow. He had always had the knack of knowing when she had complained to her mother about him—and the knack of making sure she regretted doing so.

The personal shopping suite was a revelation to someone who couldn't even remember the last time she had shopped for clothes for herself. To her relief Ollie, who had earlier been torn between enchantment and excitement, surrounded by all the toys in the babywear department, had now fallen asleep in his buggy.

Her personal shopper looked as though she was around her own age, although she was wearing clothes far more fashionable and body-hugging than Annie would ever have felt comfortable wearing.

'I'll measure you first,' she announced, after she had introduced herself as Lissa.

'I've always been a size twelve,' Annie told her, causing the elegantly arched eyebrows to arch even further.

'Different designers have differing ideas of what a specific size is, which is why we prefer to take proper measurements,' Lissa informed her with a soothing smile. 'And as for you being a size twelve—I'd bet on you being closer to a size eight. A ten at the very most. We find a lot of customers experience a change in their body weight and shape post-baby—although not many of them actually drop a size without working at it. Have you any specific designers or style in mind?'

'No. That is, we're going to be living in Sicily, so I shall want clothes suitable for a hot climate—but nothing too expensive, please. I prefer simple, plain things.'

'Daywear and evening things? Will you be entertaining? What kind of social life—?'

'Oh, no—nothing like that,' Annie interrupted her quickly. 'No. I'll be spending all my time with my son. Just very plain day things.' It was hard to sound as firm as she would have liked with Lissa encircling various bits of her body with the tape measure.

'Just as I thought,' the other woman declared triumphantly once she had finished. 'You are an eight. Now, if you'd like to help yourself to a cup of coffee—' she gestured towards the coffee machine on the table '—and then get undressed and put on a robe, I shall go and collect some clothes. I shan't be long.'

She wasn't, soon returning accompanied by two other girls and a rail packed with clothes.

Two hours later Annie felt like a small and very irritating child. Even worse, she was humiliatingly close to tears. Lissa was very much out of patience with her, she could tell.

She was back in her below-the-knee A-line denim skirt, under which her cheap tights shone in the overhead lights. The skirt was worn with a short-sleeved cotton blouse that she had bought in the latter stages of her pregnancy, which covered her from neck to hip. She felt hot and uncomfortable, and she was longing to escape from the store and from Lissa's obvious irritation.

'I'm sorry,' she apologised miserably, for what felt like the umpteenth time, 'but I just couldn't wear any of them.'

She had, she recognised, lost Lissa's attention—and the reason for that was because Falcon had just walked into the room.

'All done?' he asked, quite plainly expecting that it would be.

Annie had to say something.

'Well, not really…' she began—only to have Falcon frown.

'Why not?' he demanded.

'It seems that everything is "too revealing",' Lissa answered smartly for her, very plainly wanting to voice her sense of irritation and injustice.

Annie couldn't blame her. The clothes Lissa had shown her were beautiful—sundresses in perfect colours for her skin, with tiny straps and softly flowing skirts, well-cut narrow-legged Capri pants in white and black and zingy lime, and a shade of blue that almost matched her eyes, strappy tops, sleeveless V-necked dresses… Clothes meant to allow as much sun as possible to touch the skin. Clothes that would catch the male eye. Clothes that women wore when they wanted to attract male attention. In amongst them had been swimsuits and bikinis, wraps, sandals with no heels and high heels, underwear in cotton so fine that it was transparent—everything that any woman could reasonably need for a long sojourn in a hot climate. But Annie had rejected it all. Even the heavenly white sundress with embroidered flowers that had—ridiculously, given its sophistication—reminded her of a dress she had had when she'd been about six years old.

'Too revealing?' Falcon looked at the rack of clothes that the salesgirl was now gesturing to with her hand. He was Italian, and an architect by training and desire. Good lines were important to him, and he couldn't see anything in the clothes he was being shown that in any kind of way merited the description 'too revealing'.

He turned from the clothes to Annie, his eyebrows snapping together as he studied her appearance in the over-large dull top and the denim skirt, his frown deepening in disbelief as he realised that she was wearing thick-looking tights.

'The temperature can rise above forty degrees centigrade in Sicily in the summer. You will need clothes that are cool and loose. It will be impossible for you to continue wearing the kind of clothes you are wearing now.' He turned to the salesgirl and told her firmly, 'We will take everything.'

Everything? All of it? He couldn't mean it. But quite patently he did.

Was this how things were going to be from now on? Was he going to continually tell her what she could and could not do? Automatically she stiffened in rejection of allowing that to happen. Perhaps she had acted too impulsively and in doing so had jumped from the frying pan into the fire? Perhaps…?

'We need go get moving. My brother has arranged for one of his fleet of jets to fly us out to Sicily in four hours' time, so I suggest that we now return to your flat. I have spoken with the council, by the way, and cancelled your tenancy.'

'Cancelled it? But what if I change my mind and I want to bring Ollie back?'

'Back to what? Your stepbrother rang my office this morning, and left a message for me asking if I had managed to trace you as yet.'

Had he told her that deliberately, to put her off insisting that she might want to come back? Was he trying to manipulate her? Had she made a terrible mistake?

How her mood now contrasted with and mocked the gratitude she had felt towards him last night. Why was she such a fool? Her mother had often said that Annie was a bad judge of character. Those had been her words to Annie as she had shaken her head over a boy from university who had asked her out, and over Rachel, a schoolfriend her mother had said was a bad influence on her. And clearly she had misjudged the extent of Antonio's malice towards her, and what it would lead him to do.

She had made more than enough mistakes, enough bad judgements, and had paid the price for doing so. She wasn't going to let Falcon Leopardi browbeat her into making yet another mistake.

She lifted her chin and challenged him. 'What will you tell him?'

'Nothing. He is your stepbrother, and so it is up to you to decide what you do and do not want him to know.'

His answer took the wind out of her sails, completely deflating the hard bubble of anger inside her and leaving her feeling foolish.

'I'll have you dropped off at your flat, so that you can pack everything that you want. Don't bother about packing any baby stuff. I've phoned Rocco and asked his wife to order everything you're likely to need to be ready for you. You'll need your passport, of course. I don't expect you have one for Oliver, so I've arranged for the British passport office to get one rushed through. They'll need a photograph, needless to say, so we'll get that done now, and we can go before I drop you off.'

Falcon had thought of everything, Annie admitted tiredly later, when the chauffeur-driven Mercedes limousine came to a halt on the runway, only a matter of yards from where a sleek jet was waiting for them.

The last time Annie had flown anywhere had been when she had gone to Cannes with Susie and Tom, in her capacity as Tom's researcher. He had been attending the showing of a film based on one of his books, as well as using the trip to source some background information on his new book, set against the backdrop of the jet set. That was why she had been on Nikki Beach—because Tom had felt that she could get a better insight into a woman's perspective of the scene there than him. She had tried to protest that she wasn't that kind of researcher, and that she preferred working amongst the books of the British Library, but Tom had refused to listen.

He had been devastated after what had happened to her, blaming himself until she had begged him not to do so. Both he and Susie felt that it was for the best that she couldn't remember anything of what had happened after she had swallowed her drugged drink until she had started to come round, when Susie had found her, but Colin didn't share that view. He had pressed her over and over again, insisting that she *must* remember something.

He had never known anyone whose eyes were so extraordinarily expressive when she didn't realise she was being watched, Falcon acknowledged. He could see quite clearly the pain and fear darkening them, and he wondered who or what had caused them.

'Let me take Oliver for you,' he offered, reaching for the now awake baby as the chauffer opened the car door.

Immediately Annie recoiled, holding her baby tightly.

'I can manage, thank you,' she said, stiff and uncompromising.

She was very protective of her child, Falcon admitted, and told her dryly, 'I *am* his uncle.'

'And I am his mother,' Annie pointed out, quickly and defensively.

'You will find that in Italian families it is expected that babies are passed around amongst the relatives, so that everyone in the family can share in the joy of having them there,' Falcon informed her calmly.

Stupidly, his words made her eyes sting with emotional tears. There was nothing she wanted more for Ollie than a large and loving family who would take him to their hearts and accept him and love him. And her with him?

The chauffeur helped her out of the car, and a uniformed steward came forward from the plane to greet them, followed by the pilot. Neither of them seemed curious about her. Too well trained, Annie decided. They were probably used to Falcon Leopardi boarding private jets with a woman in tow. But not a woman like her, Annie thought, uncomfortably aware of her shortcomings. Falcon's women would be soignée and confident. They would wear designer clothes that showed off the sensuality of their bodies. They would definitely not be dressed as she was, nor holding his disliked late half-brother's child.

What was she doing, comparing herself to them? The type of woman Falcon dated and Annie Johnson were worlds apart—so very many worlds apart. Suddenly out of nowhere she felt a sharp stab of almost physical pain for all that she had lost, all that was denied to her. It was so intense that it almost made her cry out loud. *Was* there a woman in his life? A special woman? A woman who he planned would ultimately bear his children? The pain intensified, seizing her in its claws and mauling her so badly that she almost cried out.

What was the matter with her? She had everything she wanted. The sexuality and happiness of some unknown woman meant nothing to her. Her life was what it was. It was for Ollie's sake and not her own that she had even felt what she had, she defended herself. Because he would never know what it was to be the child of two people who had created him out of their love for one another, who were there with him to show him that love. She knew what it was like to grow up without a father, and she hated knowing that Ollie would suffer that same loss.

'Let me take him now.' Falcon reached for Ollie, taking from her before she could stop him, and leaving her no option other than to allow the steward to guide her up the steps and into the plane.

She tried not to be impressed, but it wasn't easy. She had never imagined that the interior of a plane could be like this—furnished more like a sitting room than the kind of aircraft interior with which she was familiar.

Falcon had followed her into the plane, and was pointing out to her the sky cot that had been prepared for Ollie. The baby was wide-awake now, and gazing round in wide-eyed delight.

He really was the most beautiful baby, Annie thought on a wave of love. She had dressed him in one of his new outfits—little chinos, with a blue and green checked shirt and a V-necked pullover, matching socks encasing his small baby feet. He looked adorable, and she suspected he knew it. She, on the other hand, was still wearing her dull top and her denim skirt—although she had put on her trenchcoat, as well, even though the early evening was mild and dry.

Oh, yes, his new family were bound to love Ollie she decided after the steward had discreetly shown her how to fasten herself into her armchair-like seat and they had begun to take off.

They would love *him* but how would they feel about *her*? How much did they know about her?

She was worrying about something, Falcon thought as he watched the now familiar darkening of her eyes. Although obviously it wasn't her appearance. He had never known a woman less concerned about how she looked. Antonio's drunken friend had mentioned her buttoned-up appearance, but Falcon hadn't paid much attention to his description until now. What made a young and potentially very attractive woman dress in such a way?

The seatbelts sign went off and Falcon unfastened his. What did it matter what motivated her to dress the way she did? It was her child who was his concern, and the duty he owed was to him. But what about the duty he owed *her*, being the brother of the man who had abused her?

Annie couldn't contain her anxiety any longer. Her fingers trembled as she unfastened her seatbelt and leaned towards Falcon Leopardi.

'Your brothers and their wives—what…what do they know about me?' she asked, her body tense with her anxiety.

'They know that you are Oliver's mother and that he is a Leopardi,' he answered her.

Colour now stained her skin, but she ignored it, pressing him determinedly, 'Do they know how I came to have Oliver? Do they know…?'

'That Antonio drugged and then raped you?' Falcon finished for her.

His voice was harsher than he had expected, scored by everything he felt about his late half-brother, and his loathing of the damage he had done to their family name, but to Annie his harshness was an indictment of her, and she flinched from it.

'Yes, they know,' Falcon confirmed.

Before he had even found her he had told them what he had discovered, and that it was his intention to find the woman Antonio had so badly wronged and bring her child within the protection of their family.

Annie's immediate gasp alerted him to her reaction.

'They know and they share my views on the subject,' he elaborated with deliberate emphasis.

'Because you have told them to?' Her voice wobbled, betraying very easily, Annie thought, what she was really feeling, and how apprehensive she was about meeting his family and being judged by them.

Falcon, though, seemed oblivious to what she was thinking, because he asked bluntly, 'What is it you are trying to say?'

'Isn't it obvious? Your brother denied that—what happened. He refused to accept that Ollie was his. How do I know that your brothers and their wives accept what really happened?' When he didn't speak she added wildly, 'Do you think I *want* people knowing what happened to me? Do you think that I *want* Ollie to grow up with people knowing how he was conceived? It was bad enough that Susie and Tom knew even before—' She broke off, suddenly realising that she was saying far more than she had intended.

Her anguished outburst brought to the surface issues Falcon had already considered and then put to one side to be dealt with once he had dealt with the most urgent necessity— which had been to find Antonio's victim and her child.

It would have been hard for her to speak as she had, he acknowledged, and something inside him ached for her whilst at the same time registering her bravery.

His brothers had already discussed with him their concern over Oliver being Antonio's child, and what he might grow up to be.

'The last thing we want is another Antonio,' Rocco had told him bluntly. 'And if our father has his way, that is exactly what he will turn the boy into.'

'I shall not allow that to happen,' Falcon had assured him. 'The child will receive his fathering from me.'

Both his brothers had looked at him in such a way that he had felt obliged to continue.

'I know what you are thinking. My fathering of both of you contained more good intention than it did skill.'

'You are wrong, Falcon,' Rocco had responded. 'What we are thinking is that there could be no one better to parent this child than you. We are both eternally grateful to you for all that you did for us.'

It had been an emotional moment, and one that still moved him. He had been so young when their mother had died and their father had remarried—too young in many ways to shoulder the responsibility of protecting his younger brothers.

'Admit it, Falcon,' Rocco had teased him, in an attempt to lighten the mood, 'you want to have this boy under your wing because you miss having the two of us there. You should find yourself a girl to love, brother—marry her and produce sons of your own to father.'

Sons of his own.

Falcon had seen his mother wilt and then turn her back on life beneath the burden of being the wife of the head of their family. And then he had seen his father's second wife glory greedily in that position, revelling in the wealth and power of her status. He envied his brothers their marriages, and the love they so obviously shared with their wives, but their situation was not his. His personal desires must always come second to his duty. Ultimately he would be the head of the family, and it would be his duty to take the Leopardi name forward into the future.

If he married then his wife would have to understand and share his goals, and acknowledge the fact that his duty would always be a third presence in their marriage. He doubted that it was possible to find a woman with whom he could share true love and who at the same time would understand his ultimate role as Prince.

He looked at Annie, who by his own actions he had now made a part of his responsibilities.

'You speak as though you fear being shamed,' he told her evenly. 'But it was Antonio who should have borne that shame. It is we who bear it now, as his family. Not you. It is for us—for me as the eldest—to see to it that Antonio's shame does not contaminate either you or Oliver. You have my word that my brothers feel exactly as I do.'

It was impossible for her not to believe him, but he had spoken only of his brothers, Annie recognised. What of their wives? Would they look down on her and question the veracity of her version of events?

The steward appeared to ask what she would like to drink.

'Just water, please,' she answered.

There was something else that Falcon knew he had to say—since she herself had raised the issue.

'If Oliver learns to feel shame, then it is from you he will learn it if you wear it like a hair shirt—as you seem to wear your clothes.'

Anger flashed in Annie's eyes.

'There is nothing wrong with my clothes.'

'On the contrary, there is a great deal wrong with them for a woman of your age.'

His forthright response left Annie feeling taken aback and defensive.

'Well, I like them. And I am the one who has to wear them.' Annie's voice was becoming as heated as her emotions.

'That is impossible. No woman of your age could possibly *like* such incredibly ugly garments. And I remind you that I am the one who has to look at them.'

Annie was outraged. Outraged and—although she was reluctant to admit it—hurt, as well.

'Just because the kind of women *you* favour—just because your…your girlfriend dresses in fashionable designer clothes—that doesn't mean—'

'I do not have a girlfriend.' Falcon stopped Annie's outburst in mid-flow.

He didn't have a girlfriend? Why was she suddenly feeling oddly light-headed, almost pleased? She wasn't. At least not because Falcon didn't have a girlfriend.

'The summer heat in Sicily is such that it will be impossible for you to dress as you are dressed now and be comfortable. Sicily's young women go bare-legged in the summer, and wear sleeveless tops.'

'They may do as they wish, but I prefer to wear clothes that are not revealing and do not draw attention to me.'

'To wear clothes as inappropriate as the ones you have on now *will* draw attention to you. So maybe secretly, for all that you deny it, that *is* what you want?'

'No. That's not true. It isn't true at all. The last thing I want is for men to look at me.'

Annie stood up as she spoke, so agitated and upset that all she could do was look wildly around for an escape.

Falcon hadn't meant to provoke such an extreme reaction. And so far as he knew he hadn't said anything about his own sex looking at her. But she was trembling from head to foot, her eyes huge in her delicately shaped face—huge, and haunted with something that looked like fear.

'I didn't intend to imply that you are deliberately courting male attention,' he tried to assure her, but Annie shook her head.

'Yes, you did. I suppose you think secretly that I encouraged Antonio—that I deserved what happened to me?'

The words were bursting out of her now, like poison from

a deep wound. The sound of her pain filled him with pity for her, awakening his own deep-rooted sense of responsibility towards the vulnerable, honed during the years of his youth, when he had tried to protect his younger brothers from the results of their father's lack of love for them.

He stood up himself.

'I think no such thing. I know that you were totally blameless.'

He had her attention now. Her lips parted and the hot pain died out of her gaze.

'You…' Annie gasped as the plane was suddenly buffeted by turbulence, throwing her off balance.

Falcon caught her as she stumbled and fell against his body, her cheek pressed against the pristine cotton of his shirt whilst his arms wrapped tightly around her. She could feel the strong, even beat of his heart. Her own pulse was racing ahead of it, fuelled by a mixture of panic and shock. She was feeling light-headed again, Annie acknowledged dizzily. It must be something to do with the atmosphere in the cabin—not enough oxygen or something… Or something? Perhaps something such as too much proximity to a certain man? He was wearing the same cologne he had been wearing before, its scent slightly stronger this time, because she was closer to his body.

Something kicked through her lower body. Shame, of course; it had to be that. She wasn't allowed to feel anything other than shame in a man's arms. She knew that. Her body shuddered and the arms holding her tightened around her.

'It's all right, keep still. It's only a bit of turbulence.'

It took her several seconds to recognise that the turbulence to which Falcon was referring as he murmured those words against her ear was outside the plane and not inside her body.

It was only natural that she should be wary of men, given what had happened, Falcon acknowledged. She needed his reassurance and his protection; she needed to feel safe so that she could enjoy her womanhood and her beauty. And he would provide her with that reassurance— just as he would provide Oliver with a secure home, and just as he had tried to provide his brothers with a strong protector. The instinct to give his protection to others was a deeply embedded part of his character and his destiny.

What must it be like to know that when a man's arms enfolded you like this you were safe and you could trust him? What was it like to lean your head against a man's chest and know that your vulnerability would be respected and your need answered?

Just for a second Annie allowed herself to let those questions into her thoughts—let her own response to them into her heart. Such a storm of unfamiliar feelings was surging through her, and at such a pace, that she felt too weak to move away. Something within her that was stronger than her learned fear, some deeply buried instinct, was pushing small, exploratory tendrils of new emotion and sensation through her fear with an unexpectedly powerful urgency, carrying to her feelings and needs within herself she didn't recognise. The urge to turn her head and breathe in the scent of Falcon's skin; the heavy pounding of her heart that did not have any association with fear; the aching urgency that seemed to have infiltrated and permeated every part of her body right down to its most intimate core. All of those things were new to her—and yet somehow known to her, as well.

The plane had levelled off and was flying smoothly again.

Ollie woke up and gave a small cry.

Brought back to reality, Annie tried to wrench herself

out of Falcon's hold. She was trembling violently, fear of her own reaction to him darkening her eyes.

Seeing that fear, and mistaking the cause of it, Falcon asked in disbelief, 'You are afraid of me?'

Annie couldn't speak. Guilt and shame gripped her.

'This is what Antonio has done to you, isn't it?' Falcon demanded. 'He has left you with a fear of all men.'

Annie couldn't look at him.

'You have nothing to fear from me,' Falcon told her gently as he released her. 'I give you my word on that, and I give you my word that in Sicily, on Leopardi land, you will be treated only with respect.'

Should she believe him and trust him? She wanted to. Just as she had wanted him to go on holding her? Guilt burned through her. *No!* That was not true. She had not wanted that. She had not been in danger of shaming herself by behaving provocatively.

Panic flared through her and her hands trembled as she reached for Ollie.

Silently Falcon watched her. She had felt so vulnerable in his arms. And it was because he had recognised that vulnerability and had wanted to reassure her that he had wanted to go on holding her. Nothing more.

Antonio had damaged her very badly. Like a small bird with a broken wing, she needed protection until she was fully recovered and able to fly once again.

He had thought originally that his only duty was to her child, but he had been wrong; he realised that now. She was just as in need of his care in her own way as her son. Now that he was aware of it he could not ignore that fact.

He had a duty of care towards her, and he would fulfil that duty. No matter what.

CHAPTER FOUR

THE heat of the Sicilian night wrapped round them like a moist blanket when they left the plane, and by the time they reached the waiting car Annie, in her heavy clothes, was drenched with perspiration.

'Rocco.' Falcon greeted the brother who was waiting for them with obvious affection and warmth, and the two men exchanged fierce hugs before Falcon somehow managed to catch hold of her arm before she could stop him, to draw her forward to be introduced to the tall, good-looking man standing alongside the waiting Mercedes.

She expected him to shake her hand, but instead he hugged her, enveloping her in an embrace which oddly did not have anything like the effect on her that being held by Falcon had.

He then admired Ollie, picking him up out of his buggy with such obvious expertise that all Annie's maternal fears were immediately soothed. He made her son smile widely as he held him high in the air with an expert male care that said that Rocco was familiar with the needs of a young child.

'He is a true Leopardi,' she heard Falcon saying as proudly as though Oliver was his, whilst his brother laughed and teased him.

'I can see that he has your eyes, brother.'

Somehow it was Falcon who took charge of Ollie when they got into the car, fastening him into the waiting baby seat whilst he made conversation with his brother.

The road to the *castello* was dark and winding—in contrast with the *castello* itself which was ablaze with lights.

'My wife is very anxious to meet you and welcome you,' Rocco told Annie before she got out of the car. 'She wanted to come with me tonight, but Falcon forbade it because he thought you would be too tired. She will be calling to see you tomorrow, though, and I dare say bringing our little one with her.'

He then kissed Ollie soundly on the forehead and gave him a firm hug, before passing him to Falcon who fastened him in his buggy whilst two men removed the cases from the back of the car.

She was then swept inside the *castello* and introduced to the housekeeper and two very young maids.

She had learned during the drive from the plane that Rocco and his wife lived in a villa some miles away from the *castello*, and that Rocco was a property developer, who travelled a great deal with his work, whilst Falcon's middle brother owned an airline. He apparently had his own apartment within the *castello*, but spent most of his time in Florence, which was where his business was based. What had surprised her most was learning that Falcon too had business interests independent of his responsibilities as his father's heir. He was an architect and conservation expert, who also had a home in Florence, as well as his own wing of the *castello*.

'So you don't live here all the time?' she questioned him now they were inside.

'Not normally, but you need not fear that I shall abandon you and Oliver.'

'I wasn't thinking that,' Annie lied. She didn't want him thinking that she needed him, because then he might start thinking that she had a personal interest in him—and she didn't.

'Maria has prepared rooms for you both,' Falcon told her, ignoring her fib. 'She will show you to them now.'

It was late, and she was tired—so tired that the minute she saw the huge, comfortable looking bed in the bedroom Maria took her to all she wanted to do was lie down on it.

She was a mother, though, with responsibilities. Although one brief look was enough to reassure her that the room into which her bedroom opened, which had clearly been turned into a nursery, was expertly quipped with everything Ollie could possibly need—including facilities for making and heating Oliver's bottle.

'The wife of the *signore*—she choose everything,' Maria told her in broken English.

'The *signore*?' Annie queried uncertainly, whilst trying not to look too yearningly at the waiting bed.

'Sí. The *signore* who is the brother of Signor Falcon. She will come tomorrow to see you.'

Maria must be referring to Rocco's wife, Annie recognised.

She woke up to find that someone must have come into the room earlier and left her a breakfast tray, with coffee and fruit and soft breads. They had also pulled back the curtains to allow the most glorious sunshine to stream into the room.

She got out of bed, wrapping herself in the towelling robe she had found in the bathroom the previous night, and went first to check on Ollie who was lying happily in his cot, watching the mobile hanging above his head.

She then poured herself a cup of coffee, drinking it with one eye on the open door to the nursery and the other on the view from the elegant French windows of her room, which opened on to a balcony large enough to contain a small table and two chairs, protected by railings high enough to make it safe for Ollie.

Already it was hot. The sky was a brilliant matt blue and the realisation that she could see the sea beyond the walls of the *castello* thrilled her with delight. Directly below the balcony were formal gardens enclosed by ancient walls over which roses climbed and tumbled. In the distance, beyond the walled garden, jagged mountain peaks rose up to meet the sky, their lower slopes cloaked in what looked like olive groves.

She could hear Ollie gurgling to himself. Finishing her coffee, she started to smile. It would be wonderful to be free to be with him and enjoy his every small development. He had loved nursery, but she had envied the nursery carers. She just hoped he wouldn't miss his little companions too much.

An hour later, with Ollie bathed, changed, fed and dressed and safely in his playpen, she went to get dressed herself. Her confusion when she couldn't find the clothes she had been wearing when she had arrived at the *castello* last night turned to suspicion and then an anger so intense that it made her shake from head to foot. She discovered that not only were last night's clothes missing, but that the suitcase containing the rest of her own things was missing, as well.

Her clothes had gone. Taken away, no doubt, on Falcon's orders, so that she would be forced to wear the clothes he had bought for her—clothes which he deemed more suitable and which—surprise, surprise—were not missing.

She would not have his choice imposed on her. She would not be bullied and controlled. But she had no option other than to wear one of the new outfits or remain in her bedroom, since she most certainly could not go downstairs wearing a bathrobe.

She could not bear to look at herself. She would *not* look at herself, Annie decided as she tugged up the zip of a pair of cotton Capri pants and slid her bare feet into a pair of pretty flat shoes. At least she'd managed to find a long-sleeved cotton wrap to wear over the strappy top she'd been forced to wear. Against her will she caught sight of her pale skin, its paleness making it look very bare.

Picking up Ollie, she hurried towards the bedroom door.

She was not going to put up with being controlled like this—and the minute she found Falcon she was going to tell him so.

The *castello* seemed to be a warren of long corridors, and she had been too tired last night to pay much attention when Maria had shown her upstairs to her room. When she had still not found the stairs, after traversing what felt like miles of corridors that led to dead ends, Annie was beginning to panic—until she turned a corner to find that she had finally reached a large landing from which the stairs swept downwards into an imposing hallway.

She was just about to go down when a door opened further along the landing and Falcon came out.

'I want my own clothes back,' Annie told him angrily, before he could speak. 'I suppose you thought you were being very clever, arranging for them to be taken away, knowing that I'd be forced to wear what you bought me. But—'

'Your clothes are missing? The ones you arrived in?'

Annie had to fight to suppress a desire to grind her teeth.

'You know perfectly well they are—and my case, as well. *You* are the one who arranged for them to be taken, You, after all, are the Leopardi heir.'

Ignoring her sarcasm, Falcon held out his hands for Ollie.

'You are wrong in your accusations. I have given no orders concerning your clothes whatsoever. Nor would I do. Personally I think that you will be far more comfortable in what you are wearing now, but the right of choice is yours. However, I think I know what may have happened to those you were wearing. Although, I have no knowledge of the whereabouts of your case. Come with me, please.'

Somehow or other he had managed to take Ollie from her, despite the fact that she had not intended to allow him to do so. Ollie certainly didn't seem to mind, beaming delightedly at his new relative and chattering away to him in his own brand of baby talk as Falcon strode down the stairs and across the hallway, leaving Annie to hurry to catch up with him.

From the hall he led her through several overpoweringly formal reception rooms, furnished with what Annie guessed must be priceless antiques, finally coming to a halt in a more comfortable-looking room where Maria was overseeing one of the maids.

The minute the housekeeper saw Ollie she beamed at him, and then greeted Annie herself.

'Annie wishes to know what has happened to the clothes she arrived in last night,' Falcon told Maria, speaking slowly and carefully in English.

Maria beamed Annie a wide smile.

'I take them and put them in the machine,' she told her with delight. 'You like coffee now? And some food?'

'We'll have coffee on the terrace, thank you, Maria,' Falcon answered. 'Oh—and you had better bring extra cups for Rocco and his wife. They should be joining us soon.'

'You will have to blame my sisters-in-law for the absence of your clothes,' Falcon told Annie as soon as Maria and the maid had left. 'They insisted on revamping the *castello*'s kitchens, with the result that Maria cannot resist using the new washing machine, on the slightest excuse. As for your case—I shall make further enquiries.'

Annie felt mortified. It was blindingly obvious that she had jumped to the wrong conclusion. If she wasn't careful, he was going to start thinking she was paranoid. Despite the fact that the interior of the *castello* was a comfortable temperature, Annie could feel perspiration breaking out on her skin. The last thing she wanted was him asking questions about her reaction to the absence of her own clothes.

'I must apologise—' she began stiffly.

Falcon shook his head to stop her continuing.

'There is no need,' he told her. 'The fault is mine, in that I obviously made you feel under pressure with advice that was unsolicited.'

Annie was so astonished by his admission that she looked up at him, her gaze mutely questioning his in an act of openness that was so alien to her that the realisation of what she was doing caught at her breath. Allowing him to see what she was thinking, allowing herself to be vulnerable—these were acts she had thought she had trained herself not to risk a long time ago.

'Until they married, and I relinquished what I'd believed

was my responsibility for their emotional well-being, my brothers berated me for my over-developed big brother concern for them. It was a habit I had fallen into when they were young, when the three of us were vulnerable to the moods of a stepmother who resented us and a father who did not care. If I sound self-pitying, that is not my intention. My brothers and I have led and continue to lead privileged lives.

'However, just as being their eldest brother does not give me the right to interfere in their lives, neither does my over-developed sense of responsibility give me the right to lecture you about the suitability of your clothes for Sicily's climate. I obviously went way over the top if you thought I had given Maria orders to remove your own clothes.'

There was that light-headed feeling again, Annie recognised. Experiencing it was becoming a regular aspect of being in Falcon's company.

'I probably overreacted,' Annie admitted.

The warm smile he was giving her was doing things to her heart that could have made it a contestant in an Olympic gymnastics team. Falcon was still smiling at her. He had a good smile—strong and real, with the curl of his mouth in amusement emphasising the fullness of his bottom lip. Something very reckless was spreading a dangerous heat through her lower body, its presence throwing her into frantic panic.

'My father will want to see Oliver, of course. He has a terminal heart condition which caused him to have a relapse whilst I was away. He has been very anxious that Oliver should become part of the family. He knows you are both here, and that has put his mind at rest, but his doctor has recommended that he needs to rest a little more before he sees the little one.

'I should warn you that my father idolised Antonio. He knows nothing of the circumstances surrounding Oliver's conception. He will not hear a word against his favourite son, and in view of his condition I thought it best not to try to force him to accept the reality of what my half-brother was. I should also warn you that my father does not treat your sex with the respect he should, and that you are likely to find his attitude offensive. I assure you that his offensiveness will not be personal in any way. If you wish, I will take Oliver to meet his grandfather.'

Falcon was trying both to warn her about his father and to protect her from him, Annie recognised, but on this occasion his concern was welcome. What was it that made the difference between care that was controlling and care that instilled in her the sweet swell of inner warmth that Falcon's was doing now?

Was it a matter of degree, of intention, or was it all down to the man offering the care?

Annie was relieved when the sound of other voices prevented her from pursuing her thoughts.

The couple coming into the hall quite plainly had so much love for one another that Annie felt a small lump of envy lock her throat. She saw the looks Rocco Leopardi was exchanging with his wife as together they strapped a happily smiling little boy who looked Ollie's age into a buggy.

Immediately the children saw one another, neither had eyes for anyone else.

'It's amazing, isn't it, how even small babies are drawn to one another? How they communicate their interest in one another without a word being said?' Rocco's wife laughed. 'I'm Julie, by the way,' she introduced herself, leaving the buggy with Rocco to come over and hug Falcon warmly, and then give Annie herself a briefer but still warm hug before admiring Ollie.

'Well, you'd certainly know that he is a Leopardi.' She laughed, adding, 'Oh, look at that, Rocco—you were right. He does have Falcon's eyes.'

'You must have been shocked when Falcon first made contact with you. I was terrified when Rocco did with me. I thought he was going to try and take my nephew away from me.'

The two women were sitting together on the terrace whilst the babies played happily on rugs at their feet. Falcon and Rocco had disappeared to attend to some family business, and in the hour during which they had been gone Annie had learned a huge amount from Rocco's wife—including the fact that at one stage the Leopardi family had thought her nephew, Josh, might be Antonio's son.

'It's very courageous of you to come here. I know how vulnerable and alone you must have felt after Oliver was born. But you've got Falcon to protect you both now, and you can trust him to do exactly that. He is honourable and strong. Rocco pretends not to, but I know that secretly he puts Falcon on a pedestal—and when you know how Falcon protected and looked after his younger brothers when they were growing up it's easy to understand why. Their father was dreadfully unkind to them, you know, and to their mother. Rocco says that it's only Falcon's sense of duty to the Leopardi name that keeps him on speaking terms with his father.

'What I admire him for most of all, though, is the way he taught his brothers to value their individuality. He encouraged them to become independent of him and of the Leopardi wealth and status. All three of them are successful in their own right, and Rocco says that is because Falcon showed them by example the importance of earning self-respect. It must have been so hard for him. After all, he was only very young himself when their mother died after Rocco's birth—not even in his teens.

'You're obviously very fond of him.' Annie smiled.

She badly wanted a change of subject. Hearing about Falcon's childhood, imagining him as a boy, hearing about his emotional pain, was bringing her own emotions too close to the surface.

'I am, yes, and I want to reassure you that you can trust Falcon, that you and Oliver will be safe in his care.' She frowned and adjusted the folds of her skirt, then played with the sunglasses she had removed and put on the table, plainly not quite at ease. 'I don't like being disloyal, but I've already told Rocco how I feel. Whilst you can trust Falcon one thousand percent, I would warn you to be wary of the old Prince. I don't know if Falcon has told you anything about their father?'

'He's told me that he idolised Antonio,' said Annie.

Julie nodded her head.

'Yes, he does. I don't think there's anything he wouldn't do to have Antonio's son growing up here, where Antonio grew up.'

There was a warning in the other woman's words, Annie felt sure. But before she could ask her more directly what it was, Falcon and Rocco had returned.

CHAPTER FIVE

ANNIE grimaced to herself as she felt her body's reluctance to return to the heavy and uncomfortable constriction of her own clothes, washed and returned by Maria, after the freedom of wearing lighter things for two full days.

The only occupants of the *castello* were the old Prince, Falcon and the servants—so surely it was safe enough for her to continue to wear her new clothes? Playing with Ollie in a shady part of the garden, she had actually felt so safe that she had even removed her wrap top.

Rocco's wife's words had gone a long way to reassure her that she could trust Falcon, and had boosted her confidence in her own judgement. Once she had settled in properly, Julie had promised, she would take her round and show her something of the island. She'd said how delighted she was that Josh, her nephew—now her and Rocco's adopted son—would have another child to play with.

'It'll be lovely to have another woman with whom I've so much in common so close,' Julie had told her warmly.

Annie hoped that they would become friends. Having friends had always been so difficult for her at home and even at university, since she had still been living at home and her mother had always been so anxious about her mixing with the 'wrong kind' of people.

It had only been after the shocking accidental deaths of her mother and her stepfather in a minibus crash whilst they had been on safari that she had finally moved away from home, helped by one of her university lecturers to get a job in London at the British Library. She had been lucky enough to rent a room in a house owned by a widow—but that, of course, hadn't been anything like as much fun as proper flat-sharing with other girls.

As it was, Colin had been concerned for her, reminding her that her mother had left the house and the responsibility for her welfare to *him*. They hadn't exactly fallen out over her decision to move to London, but Colin had let her know that her decision had upset him.

It had been a shock for her to return home from work one day to find him sitting in her landlady's front room, drinking tea with her, having—as he'd told Annie—explained to Mrs Slater that Annie's mother had made him promise that he would always keep an eye on her.

'Annie has a tendency to get involved with the wrong sort,' Colin had continued. 'Young men who aren't the type a mother wants to see her daughter associating with.'

Annie's face burned now, remembering the humiliation and her sense of helplessness at being trapped by his judgement, unable to escape from it as she had sat there listening to him.

Half-heartedly, she started to reach for her old clothes. Her case had now been found. It had been placed in a storeroom—no doubt because of its shabbiness, she suspected. However, now having been reunited with her own clothes, Annie discovered—guiltily—that she had no real wish to wear them. They reminded her of Colin. She had chosen them because of him.

The sun was striking hot bars of sunshine across the polished wooden floor and the silky antique rug that covered it. As she moved the sunlight touched her arm, gilding her skin. Julie had the most lovely light tan. Her skin, like her eyes, almost seemed to glow with good health and happiness. Her own skin looked washed out and almost sickly pale in comparison.

Julie was so obviously happy and in love. Her happiness shone from her. She had confided to Annie that she and Rocco were now expecting their own child.

'Our second child,' she had made a point of saying to Annie as she'd hugged her nephew lovingly.

What must it feel like to be so happy and have the confidence to know you had a right to be the person you were, that no one would try to change you?

More than anything else what she wanted for Ollie was for him to grow up with that freedom, and in the knowledge that he was loved. She wanted him to have confidence and to know joy.

Before she could change her mind she dressed quickly in another of her new outfits—a pretty sundress with a neatly cut square neckline, the blue cotton edged with white. The dress was decorated with a row of white buttons that ran down the front, all the way to its dropped waistline. Annie looked at the little cardigan she had put on the bed to cover her arms, and then determinedly put it back in the drawer.

Ollie had now been introduced to his grandfather—who, Annie had sensed immediately, was not in the least bit interested in *her*. She had not taken to him at all; espe-

cially when he had wept emotionally over her baby, referring to him as the son of his own best beloved son.

She hadn't been able to stop herself from looking at Falcon
when the old Prince had spoken of his preference for Antonio,
but it had been impossible to gauge what Falcon was thinking or feeling from the shuttered harshness of his face.

She had just reached the hallway with Ollie when
Falcon appeared from one of the formal reception rooms
opening off the hall, announcing when he saw her, 'Ah—
good. I was just about to ask Maria if she knew where you
were. Can you spare me a few minutes?'

'Of course.' Annie smiled. She felt more relaxed with
him now that Julie had assured her that she could trust him,
but not relaxed enough not to flinch when he put his hand
under her elbow to guide her towards the terrace.

It wasn't the first time she had reacted with betraying
intensity to either his touch or his proximity, and she could
feel him looking at her—although to her relief he didn't
say anything.

He was formally dressed in a summer-weight tan-
coloured suit and a striped shirt. His clothes somehow em-
phasised his lean masculinity, making her stomach
muscles tighten in response to the female awareness of him
that a few days ago would have sent her headlong into
panic but which now had become so familiar that she was
able to control the urgency of her need to escape from what
she was experiencing. It meant nothing other than that she
knew Falcon was a very masculine and sexually powerful
man. She was allowed to recognise that fact after all.

Once they were sitting down, and one of the maids had
brought them coffee, and Oliver was happily engrossed in
trying to roll over on his blanket, Falcon spoke.

'Since the *castello* is now to be yours and Oliver's home, we need to discuss providing you with something more comfortable and suitable than the two rooms you are occupying at the moment.'

'Our rooms are fine,' Annie assured him, but Falcon shook his head.

'No. I have my own apartment within the *castello*, my father has his rooms, and it is important that you too have somewhere that is your own—where you can make a proper home for yourself and Oliver. Besides, ultimately there will come a time when you may well want to entertain friends here privately. You are after all a young woman, and it is only natural that one day you will meet a man…'

Annie was so agitated that she would have stood up and run out of the room if it hadn't been for the fact that she couldn't leave Oliver.

'I don't want to meet a man. I will never…' She was too upset to be able to continue to speak, but Falcon could guess what she must be thinking.

'What my half-brother did was unforgivable, but you cannot let his behaviour deprive you of the right to enjoy your womanhood. If you do, you will be allowing him victory. And besides, you have Oliver to think of. I don't wish to lecture you, but I have seen at first hand the effects that my own mother's victimisation by our father has had on the emotional development of my brothers and I. It can be hard to recognise love as an adult when one has not witnessed it as a child. I fully intend to provide Oliver with a male influence in his life, but that cannot replace what he would learn from living with two people who love one another. I know that letting go of the horror of what

Antonio did to you and learning to trust my sex again demands courage, but I believe that you have that courage.'

Annie couldn't let him go on. To do so would be unfair and dishonest. His comments about the duty she owed Ollie had hit home very sharply indeed. After all, she knew all about the long-lasting effect of emotional damage that could be caused in childhood. She sat down again, folding her hands together in her lap so that he wouldn't see how badly they were shaking. She couldn't look at him. She knew if she did that she'd never be able to get through saying to him what honesty compelled her to say.

'I… It isn't just because of what Antonio did to me that I don't want to meet anyone.'

Falcon studied Annie's downbent head. There was absolutely no mistaking the intensity of her reaction.

Suddenly he was very sharply aware that he had walked into a potential minefield and must tread extremely carefully indeed.

Mentally he rapidly reviewed everything he knew about her, double checked it, and then said as casually as he could, 'It seems to me that someone must have given you your dislike of men. Perhaps you didn't like it when your mother remarried—which is not an uncommon reaction after all? You were twelve at the time, as I recall. A difficult age for us all. If your stepfather wasn't kind and understanding…'

'No.' Annie shook her head fiercely. 'No. That was not the case. In fact, both my stepfather and Colin were…they were both very kind. Colin especially.'

Colin. Colin her stepbrother. The man Falcon had disliked so very much on sight and who had been so insistent that Falcon informed him if he managed to track Annie down. Immediately and instinctively, with a gut-twisting kick of certainty, Falcon knew exactly who had damaged her beyond any kind of doubt!

'It's because of your stepbrother, isn't it?'

'No!'

Now Falcon could hear the fear in her voice.

She was on her feet, her agitation ten times stronger than it had been before, her hand beating the table as she reinforced her denial with another forceful 'No!' that sent her cup of coffee flying, soaking into the skirt of her dress.

Falcon reacted immediately demanding, 'Are you all right? Has the coffee scalded you? It was hot.'

Annie could see Falcon coming towards her, snatching up the bottle of water that had been on the table as he did so. Another minute and he would be touching her, and she couldn't bear that now—she really could not.

'No...' She drew out the word like a frightened child, holding out her hands to keep him at bay.

'It's all right, Annie,' Falcon told her calmly. 'I won't touch you or come near you, I promise. But I need to know if you have been burned.'

His voice was so calm that it brought her back to reality and sanity.

'No. I'm fine.'

'Good. Now, can we sit down and talk?'

Talk about what she had just said—what she had just admitted, he meant. Annie knew that. She was beginning to feel slightly sick and uncomfortably light-headed. She tried but could not stop herself from looking anxiously over her shoulder towards the doors leading on to the terrace.

Again Falcon realised that he could interpret her thoughts as clearly as though she had spoken them.

'Colin can't hurt you here, Annie,' he assured her. 'He won't ever hurt you again. Because I won't let him.'

Her mouth trembled as she sat down and told him, in a mechanical voice, 'He'll tell you that I'm a liar, and that all he wants to do is protect me. He'll tell you that I make the wrong kind of friends, just like he had my mother.'

The past was threatening to drag her back into its possessive embrace. Heroically, Annie pushed it away. She wasn't a child or a teenager any more. She was an adult. Falcon was watching her, quite plainly awaiting a proper explanation. There was no point in trying to pretend to him that there was no reason for him to require one. Not now, after what she had already betrayed.

'I know what you must be thinking,' she acknowledged. 'But it wasn't like that. There was never anything sexual about…about the way Colin spoke to me or behaved towards me. It was just that he was… Well, he called it being protective, but to me it felt as though I was being smothered. There wasn't anything he was doing that was *wrong*, and it was hard for my mother to understand. She thought I was being difficult and unreasonable. I'd just started senior school, and I was making friends, but Colin insisted on meeting me from school. I had one particular close friend, but he didn't like her. There was nearly an accident. She was on her bike and he was reversing his car.'

Now that she had started to speak the words wouldn't be stemmed, and the fears and doubts poured out of her in relief at the release of finally being able to speak without the fear of being reprimanded, as her mother had always done.

'I tried to tell my mother how I felt, but she liked Colin. She said that I was being difficult.'

Something about the quality of Falcon's intently listening silence made Annie look at him. The angry contempt she could see in his eyes made her flinch.

'You think the same as my mother. I can see it from your expression—' she began, only to have him cut across her.

'My *expression*, as you call it, is for your mother,' he said harshly. 'Your stepbrother may not have touched you sexually, but his behaviour towards you was abusive.'

Falcon believed her. He understood. He was taking her side.

A huge dizzying wave of relief and gratitude surged through her. *You can trust Falcon,* Julie had told her, and now Annie knew that to be true. She *could* trust him. For the first time in her life there was someone prepared to listen and understand and believe her.

'It can't have been easy for my mother.' Annie felt duty-bound to defend her parent. 'She was grateful to Colin for accepting us both in his father's life, I suppose. He often used to say to me that his father would never have married my mother if he hadn't wanted him to. My mother was the kind of woman who needed someone to lean on. She'd been very angry with my father for dying, and sometimes I felt that she wished she didn't have me—that it would have been easier for her to remarry if she didn't have a child.'

Deep down inside himself Falcon was aware of the most extraordinary sense of rapport stretching between them. He didn't like talking about his own childhood, and rarely did so, but now—with Annie—inexplicably it felt both natural and easy to do so. Because he wanted to help her—not because he needed to share his own pain, he assured himself, as he told her quietly, 'It's hard for a child to come to terms with the fact that the person who should love them the most does not do. It makes it very difficult for them to recognise and accept love as adults. My brothers have both been lucky in that respect, meeting women who are prepared to help them recognise what love is.'

'I think they were also lucky in having *you* to love and protect them,' Annie found herself saying hesitantly, but very truthfully.

It was a new experience for her to be able to speak honestly about what she thought and felt—an empowering freedom after years of having to cautiously monitor what she said, as well as what she did, in case Colin pounced on it and used it to accuse her of some fresh wrongdoing.

His brothers had had him, Falcon acknowledged, but for Annie there had not been that all-important older someone to give her a true sense of her right to be loved and valued, to show her what true self-esteem was. That was a lack they shared, and he knew very well the effect that lack could have.

'Your stepbrother treated you very badly.' It was all he could trust himself to say to Annie.

'It probably wasn't all Colin's fault,' Annie felt bound to say. 'I probably was difficult. Sometimes teenagers are. But…but when he started to criticise me, telling me what I should and shouldn't do, what I should and shouldn't wear, warning me about…about the consequences of my behaviour, I started to feel scared.'

Which was exactly what her stepbrother would have wanted, Falcon recognised.

The more he learned about Annie's stepbrother the more he despised and disliked the other man—and the more challenged he felt to free Annie from the prison in which her stepbrother had put her.

'It was the way he manipulated the truth to make it seem as though *I* was the one at fault that frightened me the most. Sometimes I even wondered if I *had* done the things he was accusing me of doing.'

'He was trying to destroy your right to make your own moral choices and judgements.'

With every word Falcon said he was lifting from her the terrible weight she had been carrying.

'Colin told my mother that I'd got in with a wild crowd at school—just because he'd seen me giggling with other girls and some boys when he came to collect me. It was all completely innocent, but he was awful about it. He said things that at thirteen I wasn't really able to deal with—things about boys and sex, suggesting that I was leading boys on, and that I wanted...'

She couldn't go on, but it seemed she didn't need to—because Falcon understood. She knew that because he was speaking evenly.

'He said things to you that made you feel ashamed of your sexual curiosity and of yourself?'

'Yes,' she agreed. Falcon had put it so simply, eloquently putting into words exactly what she had felt. 'He must have said something to my mother, as well, because she gave me a lecture about provocative behaviour and...and the danger of wearing provocative clothes. She took me out shopping and bought me longer skirts. I hated them, didn't want to wear them—they made me look so different to the other girls. But Colin said that if I didn't wear them it must be because I wanted boys to look at me.

'He used to come to my room at night after I'd gone to bed, and sit on the end of the bed to question me. He'd keep asking me over and over again who I talked to at school, and if I talked to any boys, if I *wanted* to talk to them. Sometimes I lied and said no, just to make him go away, but one day he'd been watching me and he knew I was lying.'

Annie started to tremble.

'It was awful. He was so cold, and yet so angry. He took the little china ornaments that I'd been collecting and threw them on the floor one by one, until they were all broken. He said that he didn't want to be angry with me but that it was my fault, because I'd lied to him. He said that all he wanted to do was look after me because he cared about me, and he didn't want boys thinking I was cheap.

'My mother was always saying how lucky I was to have such a loving stepbrother. She didn't understand. No one did. I wanted to go to university, and when I was offered a place at Cambridge, I was over the moon. But my mother started saying that she didn't think I was mature enough to live away from home, that it would be much better if I did what Colin had done and went to the local university so that I could still live at home. I know it was his idea— just as I know that the dent Colin put in the car belonging to the boy who took me to the school prom wasn't an accident at all.'

Annie couldn't have stopped the torrent of words now even if she had wanted to. 'Before she met Colin's father my mother always told me that ultimately our house, which had belonged to my father's family, would come to me. But when she and my stepfather died I found that the house had been left to Colin, and that he'd been appointed my guardian. Luckily I was well over eighteen by then, and one of my lecturers at university—I think he understood a bit of what Colin was like, because Colin had been difficult with *him* when he'd given me some extra tuition—helped me to get a job in London.

'Colin was dreadfully upset. He begged me to go back home, but I wouldn't. I knew he'd have to stay in Dorset because his business is there. It was wonderful, living and working in London. But somehow I still couldn't let myself be the person I wanted to be. Every time I looked at a pretty dress or a short skirt I'd see Colin's face inside my head, or hear his voice.' Her own voice trailed away into drained exhaustion.

Annie recognised distantly that she felt very weak and slightly dizzy—and also, more importantly, semi-shocked and unable to fully comprehend what she had done.

'I shouldn't have told you any of that.' The words slipped out before she could snatch them back.

'Because your stepbrother wouldn't like it? You shouldn't have *had* to tell me. Because none of it should have happened,' was Falcon's response.

Did she have any idea of the grim picture she had painted of a childhood ruined by the bullying tactics of her obsessive stepbrother and her own mother's apparent inability or unwillingness to recognise what was happening to her?

His own childhood and the childhoods of his brothers had been rendered miserable by their father's lack of love for them, but what Annie had gone through was something of a different order altogether.

There was a sour taste in his mouth, a male anger on her behalf in his heart, and a steely determination in his head. Annie was now a member of his extended family. In Falcon's eyes that meant that in addition to recompensing her for the damage Antonio had done to her it was also his duty to restore to her what had been taken from her.

'After what you have just told me I can well understand why you would have ignored and tried to avoid Antonio.'

'I knew that he was making fun of me by pretending to be interested in me. I didn't like him at all. Thankfully I can't remember anything about…about what happened,' Annie told him truthfully. 'When Susie—the wife of the author I was working for—found me, I was still half-drugged.'

'You never reported what had happened to the police?'

'No,' she agreed. 'I was afraid to—in case they didn't believe me.'

Because she had been told so often by her wretched stepbrother that she was guilty of promiscuity simply by being female that she was still unable to trust men to believe her or protect her, Falcon guessed.

'It was a terrible shock when Susie asked me if I could be pregnant. That had never occurred to me. Stupid of me, I know, but I just assumed that Antonio would have… Well, that he wouldn't want there to be any risk of a child.'

'As proof of what he had done, you mean? It was typical of Antonio that he didn't think of that.'

'Originally, when…when it had happened, Susie saw from my passport that I'd given Colin's name as my next of kin. I begged her not to say anything to anyone but… She meant well, I know. And when Colin arrived in London he was so concerned that naturally…'

'He worked the same trick on her that he had on your mother?' Falcon supplied for her.

Annie nodded.

'He wanted me to have a termination. He said it would be for the best. But I wouldn't. I couldn't. So then he started saying that I must have wanted it to happen. I told him that of course I hadn't, but he said that if I couldn't even remember what had happened I couldn't say that. He said that I'd probably encouraged Antonio—otherwise I'd want to get rid of his baby. I think Susie and Tom agreed with him, although they never said so.

When Ollie was born Colin tried to get Antonio to acknowledge responsibility for him—even though I'd begged him not to. When Antonio refused Colin started pressuring me to have Ollie adopted. He even managed to persuade Susie to side with him.' Annie shivered. 'I was so afraid that somehow he'd separate us.'

As he had successfully separated her from everyone else who might have loved her or helped her, Falcon recognised. 'That's why, when you…'

'That's why you agreed to come to Sicily?' Falcon completed her sentence for her.

'Yes. I thought Ollie would be safe here.'

'You thought right,' Falcon confirmed grimly.

'You must understand now why I don't want to get involved with anyone,' Annie told him tiredly.

For a few seconds she thought he wasn't going to respond. But then, when the silence had stretched for long enough to make her feel she had said the wrong thing, he asked quietly, but with open confidence in his own correct assessment of things, 'There's never been anyone special for you sexually, has there? Someone who, when you look back, you recognise as the person you shared sexual intimacy with and who gave you the foundation stone of understanding and appreciating your own sexuality?'

For some reason Annie discovered that she wanted badly to cry. She had spent so many years cut off from what it meant to be a woman that she had grown to accept it as her fate. She was alone with it, and with the secret burden of its grief. Now, with a few simple words, Falcon had shone a light on that dark secret place within her, illuminating it so brightly that the brightness hurt unbearably, making her feel that she wanted to retreat back into the safety of the dark. She felt ashamed, she recognized. Ashamed and afraid.

She couldn't answer his question. She just couldn't. The truth hurt too much, made her feel too raw and vulnerable, and yet to her own disbelief something deep inside her was struggling against her shame and her fear, making her give Falcon an answer.

'No. Never,' she heard herself admitting shakily. 'I was too young when…when Colin first started making me feel uncomfortable about…'

She had to stop now. She had already said too much, betrayed too much. It was shamefully ridiculous and humiliating that she, a woman of twenty-four, a *mother* of twenty-four, had never known what it was to experience the pleasure of good sex.

'About being attracted to the opposite sex? About liking boys and exploring the sensations thinking about liking boys aroused?'

Annie wanted to cover her ears with her hands, just as though she was still twelve years old.

'There is nothing to be ashamed of,' Falcon was telling her. 'That is how it starts for all of us. With curiosity and awareness, with excitement and a dread of making a fool of oneself.'

'I can't imagine *you* ever feeling like that. Worrying about making a fool of yourself, I mean,' Annie explained hastily. She didn't want to think about the first part of his description. It caused too much dangerous tumult inside her body, and she already had more than enough problems to deal with.

'I can assure you that I did. Everyone does. It's a natural and normal part of growing up—but you were denied that.'

'I couldn't bear the thought of someone thinking about me in the way Colin told me that boys—men—thought about women who allow them sexual intimacies. I couldn't let myself even *think* about being attracted to anyone,' she admitted.

It was disconcerting to realise how shocked and ashamed she would have been such a very short time ago to have said those things to him—things that now she could speak of so easily and openly.

'So you suppressed your natural inclinations along with your desirability and your right to your own sexuality?' Falcon prompted her.

'I just wanted to feel safe.'

'From boys, or from your stepbrother?'

Annie's eyes widened in silent recognition of how well he understood just what she had felt.

'I suppose I could have tried to…to be more normal when I came to London, but all the other young women I saw were so…so everything I knew that I wasn't. I couldn't imagine that anyone… That is to say I thought that if I did start to go out with someone, when they found out they'd either be put off or laugh at me. It seemed easier somehow not to bother. And now, of course, it's too late. I couldn't start a relationship now even if I wanted to. What man these days wants a woman like me. A single mother, who doesn't know the first thing about how to give and receive sexual pleasure, or what it's like to enjoy sex? How would I explain to them? I couldn't tell them…'

'Why not? You've told me?'

His words had her lifting her head to look at him, caught in the shock of her realisation not just of what she had done, but more importantly of how easy it had been.

'That's different,' she told him weakly. 'You aren't… We aren't… I know I can trust you because…'

Because what? Because of what he was or because of *who* he was? Annie wasn't sure. She just knew that Falcon was different, one of a kind—a man who embodied qualities that in the modern age were very rare.

'It must have been very hard for you to live as you have lived—to live—such an unnatural life for a young and attractive woman.'

Falcon thought she was attractive? Or was he just saying that because he felt sorry for her?

'You needn't feel sorry for me,' Annie defended herself. 'I'm perfectly happy as I am.'

'No, you are not,' Falcon corrected her. 'You merely think that you are happy. But you are so afraid of being punished that you have completely disowned your sexuality. That is no way for you to live—in constant denial and fear of such an essential part of yourself.' His voice had changed and become sternly autocratic.

'It is the way I *have* to live,' Annie told him. 'I don't have any other choice.'

'But you would like that choice? You would wish, if you could, to be restored to your sexuality? To be reunited with it? So that armed with it you could have the freedom and the right to find someone with whom ultimately you might share your life?'

'I…' She desperately wanted to hang on to her pride and deny that she wanted any such thing, but Falcon's words had awakened inside her such a sharply painful, yearning pang of longing for all that she could not have that it shamed her into telling him the truth. 'Yes,' she admitted.

Falcon looked away from her. He had come to a decision. It had been there all the time he had been listening to her. Initially it had been more of an awareness that had now coalesced into the decision that he now realised he had somehow known he must make right from the beginning.

'There is something I have to say to you,' he told Annie. 'Your right to your sexuality has been stolen from you by a member of my sex, and the damage that he has done has been compounded by a member of my family. As a Leopardi, and the eldest of my brothers, I have a duty to make recompense to you and to restore to you what has been taken away. That is the law of the Leopardi family and the code by which we live.'

'That's nonsense,' Annie told him unsteadily.

Something dark and steely glinted in the depths of his eyes as he turned his head to look at her.

'It is my duty,' he repeated. 'A duty I owe not just to you but to Oliver, who shares my blood. He has the right to grow up with a mother who rejoices in her sexuality instead of fearing it, and who can thus show him a good example of all that a woman who values herself should be. How can he choose a partner who is worthy of him if he does not know what to look for? It is your duty as his mother to provide him with a template for that woman.'

With every word he said Falcon was making her feel more guilty.

'It's all very well you saying all this,' she told him helplessly. 'But I can't become the kind of woman you describe.'
'Yes, you can. With me as your guide and teacher.'

CHAPTER SIX

WITH him as her guide and teacher? Did that mean what she thought it meant? Annie's heart started to thud unsteadily.

'Give me your hand,' Falcon demanded.

Reluctantly Annie held out her hand, stiffening when he took it and held it between his own.

'Five minutes ago you said to me, "What man these days wants a woman like me? A single mother, who doesn't know the first thing about how to give and receive sexual pleasure, or what it's like to enjoy sex." I believe that deep down inside you *do* want to take back to yourself what has been stolen from you, and that you *do* want to walk free as a sexually confident and happy woman. Isn't that so?'

'I don't know,' Annie answered uncertainly. Her heart was racing. She felt as though she was confronting something she knew to be dangerous but that she also found enticing and exciting.

'Yes, you do,' Falcon corrected her. 'You love Oliver, and you know that ultimately, in order to give him the right to grow up confident in his own sexuality, you need to be confident in yours. I can teach you how to be what you want to be. You said earlier that you trusted me?'

'I…'

'I promise you that you can. I promise that I will not hurt you or abuse you, or do anything that you do not wish me to do. But I also promise you that I will show you and teach you that you have the right to own your own sexuality, to take pleasure in it and give pleasure through it.'

He meant what he said, Annie recognised weakly. He was a crusader, a motivator, a man with a mission—and he meant to restore to her what she had thought was forever lost.

'If you wish, step by step, I will help you to rediscover what has been stolen from you. You do not have to accept. I would be as bad as your stepbrother if I coerced you verbally or emotionally to accept my help. All I will say to you is that you should ask yourself what you really want and be brave enough to take it. Once you have made that decision I promise that I will be here for you and with you. There won't be anything you can't tell me or ask me.'

'What you're saying is that for Oliver's sake and my own I need to learn what it is to enjoy sex. But we don't…we don't…'

'We don't what?'

'We don't *love* one another,' Annie told him.

There was a gleam in his eyes that made her heart thud as though it was flinging itself against her ribcage.

'It is not necessary to love to enjoy good sex. It *is*, though, important to share a mutual attraction.'

He paused whilst her heart somersaulted and thudded so much that she had to lift her hand to her chest, in an attempt to steady its frantic beat.

'It is my belief that we share such an attraction.'

'No…I mean, I don't think…'

'You don't think what? That I find you attractive? I assure you that I do.'

Falcon was still holding her hand, and now to her shock he turned it over, then gently ran the pad of his thumb over her inner wrist.

Lightning surges of reaction hot-wired up her arm, causing her to gasp out loud and try to pull away.

Falcon was watching her closely, and Annie knew that her reaction had been plain to him and had given her away.

'You gave me a shock,' she told him feebly. It was the truth—even if the reality was that the shock he had given her had been entirely sexually charged rather than mentally.

'I gave you pleasure,' Falcon corrected her softly. 'And your pleasure gave me pleasure. Imagine, if the touch of my thumb can give us both that pleasure, how much more intense it would be if I followed up the touch of my thumb with the caress of my lips.'

Oh, to be a Victorian virgin and free to swoon, Annie thought feverishly. Because that was the only guaranteed way she could think of escaping from her present situation. And by her present situation what she meant was the sheer extent of the feeling of longing that surged through her at the mental images Falcon's soft words had created.

'It is entirely possible to enjoy sex without loving someone, you know,' he was telling her now. 'Just so long as there is mutual respect and understanding, and a mutual desire to give and receive pleasure. There is nothing shameful in that—no matter what your stepbrother may have tried to make you think.'

He had released her hand now, and she was delighted that he had done so. Totally delighted. And relieved that he hadn't thought it necessary to show her just what the caress of his lips could do. Absolutely. Definitely.

'You don't have to make up your mind right now. I have to fly to Florence later this afternoon, for a meeting about a building I'm involved in helping to renovate,' Falcon told her. 'I shall be back by tomorrow evening. You can give me your decision then. I'm not your stepbrother, Annie. I might tell you what I think would help you, but only *you* can make the decision as to whether or not you agree with my assessment of the situation and want to accept my help.'

Annie leaned over the still, sun-warmed water of the fish pond in the middle of the formal garden, dropping in some crumbs of bread for the fat lazy goldfish and then trailing her fingers in the water. Ollie slept in his buggy. By now Falcon would be in Florence. The *castello* felt empty without him.

When he came back— Her hand jerked, disturbing the basking fish, her skin burning. She didn't want to think about his return, because that meant she would have to think about the decision she had to make before that return.

There was no decision to make, she reassured herself determinedly, standing up and taking hold of the buggy, preparing to take Ollie back inside. She was happy as she was.

She was happy as she was. Was she? Then why was she repeating those words to herself as though they were some kind of mantra she needed to use to reinforce her belief in her own words? Annie asked herself later than evening as she prepared for bed. She wanted to escape from the disconcerting pressure of the increasingly rebellious thoughts that were trying to undermine the sensible decision she had already made.

Although thankfully she had no memory of Antonio's abuse, he *had* stolen something from her. And that was her right to give her body freely to the man of her own choice for that first special time. Deep down inside it *did* hurt to know that her body's only experience of sex was such a cruel one. If she was honest, didn't she feel cheated of something very special? Of something that could have been and should have been very sweet? Nothing and no-one could give her back what she had lost, but what Falcon was offering her could be a very special gift to her body. Didn't she owe herself that for what Antonio had taken?

Falcon was man enough to offer to recompense her—was she woman enough to accept? A frisson of something that could have been dangerously close to excitement raced down her spine.

Falcon. Even his name sounded strong. *He* was strong. Strong enough to conquer her past and her pain? Could she afford to let him try?

For Ollie's sake, could she afford not to?

She felt so restless and on edge—so buoyed-up and...and filled with conflicting feelings.

It was only half past nine. No doubt in Florence Falcon's evening would only just be beginning, Annie acknowledged as she ran a bath for herself, hoping it would soothe her and help her to sleep.

Falcon might be stepping into the shower, before going out for the evening. Unbidden and definitely unwanted, out of nowhere she had a mental image of him standing beneath the shower, water cascading down onto his broad shoulders, and from there down over his chest, smoothing and flattening the dark hair on his body, running in rivulets that arrowed downwards.

Annie gasped, and tried to sink beneath the water of her bath to hide her shocked chagrin. What was the matter with her? She had never thought about a man like this before—imagining him naked, imagining him aroused, imagining that arousal giving her a feast of varied sensual pleasures. It was an imagining which now had a very real physical effect on her own body, in the tightening of her nipples and in the slow, grinding ache that had taken possession of her lower body.

What would Falcon think of her body? Would he think it attractive? Would it arouse him? Her breasts were firm and full. She had been so embarrassed when she had been the first girl in her class to need a bra—and even more un-comfortable when Colin had started asking her if boys ever tried to touch them. After that she had taken to wear-ing tops that were big and loose to disguise them.

If she accepted Falcon's offer he wouldn't expect her to do that. He'd want her to take pride in them. He'd want to see them and touch them—kiss them, perhaps. What was she doing, allowing herself to think like this? She'd already de-cided that she wasn't going to accept his offer—hadn't she?

She tried to think about something else—anything else. She didn't need to rediscover her lost sexuality. She was happy as she was. She had her adored son, and she felt she was on the verge of making a good friend in Julie. She and Rocco were so obviously happy together, and they loved one another very much. Anyone could see that. Every smile and every touch they exchanged showed their feel-ings for one another. Wouldn't *she* secretly like to be like that? To have a partner, someone with whom she shared that kind of bond of love and commitment? No, she wouldn't.

They might be lucky enough to love one another, but couples made commitments to one another every day of the week and then regretted them. She didn't need anyone else in her life, she didn't need Falcon to teach her to let go of the past, and most especially she didn't need Falcon to show her how to reawaken her suppressed sexuality. Because it was already awakening of its own accord. And she was afraid that if it awakened any more she might be in danger of enjoying her lessons way too much.

That was ridiculous.

But so was trying to lie to herself that she would be happy to spend the rest of her life alone. Everyone needed and wanted love.

She had Ollie.

Who one day would want to live his own life, find his own personal happiness. How would she feel if he was unable to do that because of her?

Her bathwater was growing cold, and her head was beginning to ache with the weight of her confused and contradictory thoughts.

Don't think about it any more.

She wasn't going to.

She stepped out of the bath and reached for a towel.

What was Falcon doing now? Was he thinking about her at all?

Why should he be thinking about her. She didn't *want* him to be thinking about her. Because if she did then that would mean…

What? What would it mean? Certainly not that she had some private ulterior motive for wanting to agree to his suggestion. Those almost forgotten frissons of sensation that had stoked her body into renewed sensual life from the first minute she had seen him meant nothing other than that her body was one step ahead of her head, that it was already eager to become the body of a woman who knew and understood her own sensuality.

Freedom was beckoning her. It was freedom that was causing such an intoxication of her senses, overwhelming the barriers of her anxiety and fear.

There was nothing personal in those unsettling little surges of sensation that pulsed through her and gripped her every time she allowed herself to acknowledge that Falcon was a very male man. It was just the same kind of natural response to a situation as the tingling that came from blood returning to numbed flesh.

Pulling on her bathrobe, Annie walked through her own bedroom and into the nursery, where Ollie lay peacefully asleep in his cot.

With a mother's instinct she knew it wasn't just her imagination that her son was thriving in his new environment. He had put on weight. And already his skin—despite the copious amounts of sun protection cream in which she smothered it—was warming to what she suspected was really its natural colour. It hadn't escaped her that the colour was closer to Falcon's skin tone than it was to her own. Already he seemed to be taking a much greater interest in his surroundings, smiling more readily at the strangers who had come in to his life than he ever had at strangers in London. Did he somehow, with his baby instinct, sense that these new people were *his* people, of *his* blood?

What she would be doing if she accepted Falcon's offer

wouldn't be so much for herself as for Ollie. Annie felt love for her baby gripping her heart. When he grew up she wanted more than anything else what surely every loving parent wanted for their child. She wanted his happiness and his joy in life. She wanted him to know and share love, and to build good relationships out of that knowledge. She wanted for him all that she had not known but must for his sake learn.

But could she do it? Could she find the strength to thrust herself into the fire and endure more, much more, of what she already felt when Falcon touched her?

CHAPTER SEVEN

'I'VE been thinking,' Falcon announced, leaning forward across the wrought iron table on the terrace, where they'd been sitting, drinking a pre-dinner aperitif.

He had arrived back from Florence just over half an hour ago. Annie had seen him drive up to the *castello* and then into the paved courtyard. She had watched him uncurl his lean height and muscular shoulders from his car, and then reach back inside it to gather up his suit jacket and a small laptop case, hooking the jacket over his shoulder before mounting the flight of marble steps that led up to the main entrance of the *castello*.

His shirt had been unfastened at the throat, just by one button, but the brilliance of the late-afternoon sun had struck through his shirt so clearly that she could almost have traced the dark shadowing of male body hair that crossed his chest and bisected his flat six-pack. There was something very sensually male about that dark shadowing. Something so strongly intimate that it had set off a reaction inside her that curled mockingly round her prim self-consciousness, silencing the voice that had said it was wrong for her to watch him and be so aware of his masculinity.

It wasn't as though she had been waiting for him to return. The only reason she had been on the first floor of the *castello*, and thus able to witness his arrival through one of the windows of the line of formal salons on this side of the building, was because Maria had insisted on giving her a tour of them.

The *castello* was enormous, with cellars and attics and three and sometimes four full floors in between. It had three towers, a huge ballroom, and was in fact a combination of the original *castello* and an eighteenth-century *palazzo* which one of Falcon's ancestors had built to extend the original building.

He'd changed out of his suit now, and was wearing a pair of faded, well-washed jeans and a soft white linen shirt, his bare feet thrust into soft shoes. He looked casually relaxed, whilst she felt tensely uncomfortable in one of her new dresses. She didn't want him to think that she had deliberately tried to make herself look more attractive for him. That wasn't the case at all. She had simply grabbed the first dress that had come to hand after he had strolled into the salon where she had been with Maria, to ask her to join him on the terrace for a drink before dinner.

Tonight would be the first time she had had dinner with him since she had come here. Previously she had eaten alone—and happily—she assured herself, in her room, content to be safe and with Ollie, and not wanting anything or anyone else.

It wasn't her fault that the dress she had grabbed turned out to be a sleeveless tube of honey-coloured jersey. It had looked so nondescript on its hanger that she hadn't given its suitability a second thought when she had pulled it on over her head, before slipping on a pair of kitten-heeled sandals. As the mother of a six-month-old baby she had no intention of wearing high stiletto heels in case she stumbled and Ollie came to harm.

She hadn't even looked at her full-length reflection before leaving her bedroom, simply running a brush through her hair and then sliding on a soft slick of lipgloss, before spraying herself with the admittedly delicious light scent the personal shopper had recommended, and scooping up Ollie.

In fact, it had only been when she had been about to leave her bedroom that she had caught sight of herself in the mirror and had realised how very slender the jersey dress made her look—how faithfully it followed the lines of her body, despite the stylish pleated ruching that swept from the bust right down to her hip, which she had naively assumed meant that the dress would be suitably unrevealing.

It had been too late to go back and get changed, but she had comforted herself with the thought that she would be sitting down and the dress's neckline, whilst slashed across her throat, did not reveal very much flesh.

That had been before she had realised that Falcon was already on the terrace and waiting for her—or realized that he would come towards her to take Ollie from her, and then survey her in such a silent and yet at the same time very meaningful way. Her heart kicked off in a flurry of little beats now, just thinking about the way he had smiled at her before he had come to put Oliver in the highchair that was pulled up at the table, waiting for him.

It wasn't the way Falcon had smiled at her five minutes ago that she ought to be concentrating on, Annie warned herself. It was what he had just said to her. What had he been thinking? That he had changed his mind about his plan to turn her into a fully functioning modern sexual woman? Of course, if that was the case she would be relieved in many ways. Very relieved. Wouldn't she?

She took a quick sip of her drink. She didn't normally touch alcohol, but the chilled light rosé wine Falcon had persuaded her to try was delicious. She could feel it relaxing her tense cramped stomach muscles as she tried to breathe evenly, as though she wasn't in the least bit apprehensive and most particularly as though she hadn't hardy slept at all last night for thinking about what he had said to her, what she would say to him, and how she felt about…about everything.

'Whilst I was in Florence I was speaking with a member of my late mother's family. One of the old family houses is currently being emptied of its treasures, including the books from its library and a great many family letters. He has asked me if we could house the books here, to which of course I have agreed.

'My mother's family history is an interesting one. They were originally silk merchants in the fifteenth century, who bought themselves into the nobility and ultimately became very wealthy and well connected. The marriage between my parents was one brokered between my father and my mother's uncle, for reasons of mutual financial benefit and social prestige. However, my father never allowed our mother to forget that, whilst his family line descended directly from nobility, hers descended from the merchant class.'

'Your mother must have been so hurt,' said Annie sympathetically.

'She suffered very badly because of my father's cruelty to her. As children we all felt that our mother must not have loved us enough to want to live, but of course that was not the reality. The reality is that she died from complications after Rocco's birth.'

Annie could see the three bereft children, desperately longing for their mother, all too easily. Her heart ached for those boys, and inside her head she saw herself as a mother, gathering them close—especially Falcon, who she knew would have been proud and brave and determined to hold back his own tears in order to comfort his brothers.

'Growing up without your mother must have been awful for you.'

'As growing up without your father must have been for *you*. The understanding of what that means is something we share. It may be that, should you decide to learn Italian, you will one day read the story of my parents' families for yourself. The library here at the *castello* holds many personal diaries.'

Immediately Annie's eyes lit up with excited anticipation.

'There's nothing I'd like to do more,' she admitted.

'Then I shall make some enquiries and find a teacher for you. Or if you prefer you could take a language course in Florence. My apartment there is large enough to accommodate you and Ollie.'

He was being so kind. Whilst she had been listening to him she had, she realised as Falcon reached for the bottle of rosé and leaned across to top up her glass, almost emptied it.

'Oh, no. No more for me. I don't drink at all normally—' she began, but Falcon ignored her and continued to pour.

'I am most certainly not in favour of anyone drinking more than they should, but it is important that you learn to drink a couple of glasses of wine without it going to your head. It will give you confidence in social situations. Now, I have also been thinking about you and Oliver whilst I was in Florence.'

Annie's heart gave another furious flurry of too-fast beats, so she took another sip of her wine. It did taste good, and a lovely warm, mellow and relaxed feeling was beginning to creep over her.

'If you are to have any quality of life of your own then you will need someone who you can trust to look after Oliver in your absence.'

'I don't want anyone else to look after him,' Annie protested. 'I love him and I want to be with him.'

'It is not healthy when mother and child have only one another. Normally in Italian families there is always someone for a mother to turn to for help. She is not left alone to bring up her child. I have spoken with Maria already, and she has a cousin who trained as a nursery nurse. She and her husband have recently returned to live on the island, and I have arranged for her to come up to the *castello* when you feel ready to speak with her. You can interview her. If you decide she is suitable then you will be doing her a favour, as well.'

Noblesse oblige, Annie thought ruefully, but she knew that what he was saying made sense, so she nodded her head and then said, 'Ollie's falling asleep. I'd better take him upstairs and put him to bed.'

Falcon's answer—'I'll carry him for you'—had her denying that there was any need for him to do so, but Falcon simply stood up and went to lift Ollie out of his chair.

'I have a distinct feeling that if I let you disappear upstairs alone you won't come back down again. And as you know we have an outstanding matter to discuss,' he told her.

Annie was glad she wasn't holding Ollie, because she suspected that if she had been she would have been in danger of dropping him, so great was the effect of Falcon's words on her.

It didn't take her long to put Ollie to bed. He was such a good baby. She smiled lovingly as she kissed his forehead, and then gave a small gasp as she realised that Falcon had come from the small sitting room that opened off her bedroom into the nursery, and was standing watching her.

'Oliver is a very lucky child to have such a devoted mother.'

Was he thinking of his own mother, and how he and his brothers as children had mistakenly felt that she had not loved them enough to fight death to be with them?

Instinctively moved to comfort him, she told him gently, 'I'm sure your mother did love you all, Falcon—and that she wanted to be with you. Even though to you as a child it must have seemed that she had chosen not to live.'

She had lifted her hand to his sleeve as she spoke, touching his arm in the kind of tender gesture that came unbidden and naturally, but now—as he moved closer to her and she felt the hard, muscular warmth of his flesh beneath her fingers—a very different feeling from the one that had originally motivated her surged through her, causing her to snatch back her hand and quickly turn towards the door, her face hot.

'You have a very compassionate nature,' she heard Falcon saying as he followed her. 'And I think you are right. Certainly as an adult it is pity I feel for my mother, rather than the despair her death caused me as a boy. She used to say that producing us was her duty and that she herself was a sacrifice.'

Annie had to fight hard not to betray her shock. Poor woman. She must have been dreadfully unhappy to have spoken to her son like that, instead of protecting him from her own unhappiness. She would never do that to Ollie. *Never!* She wanted him to grow up whole and happy, and free of any sense of guilt about her or about himself.

They had dinner. Warmed goat cheese with tomatoes and herbs to start with, and then a roast chicken and pasta dish that was mouthwateringly delicious.

Annie had already learned from Maria that most of the staff at the *castello* were local, and that their families had lived and worked on Leopardi land for countless generations—even the chef.

She had drunk another glass of wine with her meal, and now she and Falcon had finished the piping hot coffee the little maid had brought them. Although Annie had regretfully had to refuse the chocolate *petit fours* that had been with the coffee—not just because she was full, but because she was also feeling very nervous. All through the meal Falcon had answered her curious questions about the obviously feudal nature of the area, and the relationship between his father the old Prince and the people who looked on him almost as though he were still their ruler. Not once had he made any reference to the fact that she had not as yet given him her decision.

'My father's attitude towards the land and the people *is* feudal,' Falcon told her now. 'And that is a matter of great concern to me and to my brothers. We have all been fortunate in having benefited financially through our mother's family, and we have all become financially successful in the modern world. The opportunity to live in that modern world is one I am committed to giving to our people, despite my father's wish to keep them locked in the past. And speaking of people being locked in the past...' He stood up. 'A walk in the gardens will, I think, help us to digest our dinner. And whilst we are walking you can give me your decision on the offer I made before I left for Florence.'

Annie's breath escaped her lungs in a leaky gasp.

'What is it?' Falcon asked as she too stood up.

'I thought that perhaps you'd changed your mind about that, and that that was why you hadn't mentioned it,' Annie confessed.

'You thought or you hoped?' he challenged her, even as his light touch—and it was merely a touch, quickly removed—guided her towards the steps that led down into the gardens.

It was darker here than it had been on the terrace. A prickle of sensation quivered over her skin. The night was full of hidden dangers—or were they hidden promises? What on earth had made her think *that*?

The moon, new and bright, gave off just enough light to show the outline of the mountains, silvering Leopardi land, the olive groves and the fields closer to the *castello*. Her son was part of all of this—but he was part of her, as well. Somewhere unseen a bird screeched, making her jump and miss a step. Instantly Falcon moved closer to catch her, one hand splayed across the middle of her back the other encircling her wrist.

Had he turned her in towards his own body or had she done that for herself? Annie didn't know. She did know that she was acutely aware of him. She could smell the scent of his skin, its familiarity immediately transporting her back to the first time they had met.

'Are you warm enough?'

Had he felt the rash of goosebumps that had suddenly come up under her skin? He must have done. They weren't caused by cold, though. The evening air was wonderfully balmy and warm.

'It's late,' she told him unsteadily, as she looked imploringly towards the *castello*.

'Too late to change your mind,' Falcon told her.

He *had* moved closer to her—much closer. They were standing face to face. One of his hands was still splayed out across her back, its firm pressure bringing her towards him, whilst the other hand...

Annie had to swallow very hard. The fingertips of the other hand were slowly stroking her bare arm in a caress that drifted from her inner wrist all the way up to her elbow. Tongues of fire licked through her veins. She was trembling openly now, completely unable to conceal her reaction to him.

She still made a brave attempt to face him down, though, reminding him shakily, 'I haven't given you my decision yet.'

He was so close to her that she could feel his chest shaking as he laughed. The warmth of his amusement gusted round her, his breath grazing her cheek and making her turn and lift her head as though she wanted to capture it with her lips.

'Yes, you have,' he corrected her. 'You told me when I refilled your wineglass and you trembled; you told me when you looked at my mouth over dinner; just now when you shivered when I touched you. You told me then that you are ready to be aroused by me. Your body has signalled to mine its curiosity and its interest.'

Annie opened her mouth to object, to tell him that he was wrong, but the unseen bird screeched again and instead she gasped and moved closer to Falcon.

It was the wrong thing to do. His arm was encircling her now, holding her against his body, whilst her own body trembled helplessly beneath the slow caress of his fingertips on her arm.

Somehow, without her knowing what she was doing, she had gripped his other hand, curling her fingers into the muscle as she clung to him.

'How does this feel?' he asked her softly as his knuckles brushed her arm lightly.

'I don't know,' Annie lied. But of course she did. It felt shockingly and dangerously erotic.

Beneath her dress she could feel her nipples tightening, whilst heat curled through her lower body and the insides of her thighs began to ache, the feeling there spreading from deep inside her body.

She badly wanted to close her eyes and simply lean into Falcon, so that he could hold her and caress her, those magical knowing hands of his touching all those places that were now aching for his touch.

Panic hit her and she pulled back from him. Everything that Colin had told her and warned her about suddenly flooded into her head, filling her with self disgust and shock. The woman she wanted to be and the girl she had fought relentlessly with one another for possession of her mind.

Falcon had stepped back from her, his hand holding her own as he directed her deeper still into the garden. The danger had passed and she was safe. But was safe what she really wanted to be? Hadn't there been a moment back there—more than merely a moment—when she had been anticipating the touch of his mouth on her own with greedy longing?

'You are a woman it is extremely easy for a man to want,' Falcon told her.

His voice reached her out of the darkness and had her stopping, walking to turn and confront him with her emotional response.

'You don't have to say things like that to me. In fact, I would rather that you didn't. I'm not a complete fool, even if I am laughably sexually inexperienced. I know perfectly well that you're just trying to be kind and to…to boost my confidence. A man like you would never find me extremely easy to want.'

The moonlight fell directly on Falcon's face, highlighting its sensually male structure and sending a flood surge of aching, sweet need pounding through her. What was happening to her? Whatever it was it, was happening far too fast.

'By your own admission you know nothing about the needs and desires of my sex. Therefore you are not qualified to know that I would never find you extremely easy to want.' Falcon swept aside her argument, his voice sharpening as he added, 'The discovery that you have the ability to arouse me simply by doing nothing other than letting me see and feel your response to me is as unfamiliar to me as it is to you.'

'I…I'm flattered that…that you…'

'That I find you desirable? That being here in the moonlight with you arouses me? We must take things slowly if I am not to lose my head and thus lose my efficacy as your teacher.'

His face was shadowed and hidden from her now, but

Annie could tell from his voice that he was smiling—which must mean that the eventuality to which he was referring, namely him losing his head, was simply not going to happen. And that was a relief to her. Of course it was. The last thing she wanted was for Falcon to become so aroused by their intimacy that he lost control and made proper, real passionate love to her—wasn't it?

'I ought to go in. I don't like leaving Ollie on his own.'

'Don't worry, I asked Maria to keep an eye on him. I knew that maternal heart of yours would be anxious.'

Before Annie could thank him he continued.

'In a week or so's time, once you have settled in and if you are agreeable, I thought I would take a day off to show you and Oliver something of the island.'

A week or so's time seemed a safely vague distance away, so it was easy for her to say, half shyly, 'Thank you. I would like that.' After all it was the truth. She *would* like to see something of the island.

They were deep in the garden now, hidden from the moonlight by the branches of a tree, and yet Falcon still managed to find her forehead accurately as he deposited a light kiss there, and told her, 'Now you can relax. Because the first lesson is almost over.'

'I just hope you don't mean to set me any tests,' Annie responded feelingly, in her relief, and then realised her mistake when Falcon laughed.

'Oh, I fully intend to do that,' he assured her. 'And to see how much you have been paying attention to what I have been doing by getting you to repeat my caresses for you on me. But not yet.'

He was going to expect her to caress him—to send those same quivers of helpless mindless physical delight zinging through his body that he had sent through hers. Impossible!

'There is just one thing more I intend to do tonight, before I let you escape from your instruction.'

One more thing? Annie's head jerked towards him, and as though that was exactly what he had intended he cupped the side of her face with his palm and then stroked his thumb across her half-parted lips, brushing softly to and fro against them whilst her senses reeled and her mind slipped away, allowing her body and her sensuality to take control.

Falcon's arm was round her, supporting her, whilst his thumb probed between her parted lips. Without even having to think about it Annie touched his thumb with the tip of her tongue, exploring its texture and its taste, circling it and stroking it, growing bolder as she realised how powerful it made her feel to take that control.

Lost in the excitement of what she was doing, she didn't even realise at first that Falcon had removed his thumb and replaced it with his mouth until he started to kiss her.

There was no chance for her to deny him and no point, either. Her lips, she herself, were both already open to him, and to the raw sexuality of his kiss. He was cupping her face with both of his hands now, caressing her skin as he took the kiss deeper, his tongue probing the soft sweetness of her mouth whilst his fingers spread to her ears and the responsive area just behind them.

Annie heard herself moan into Falcon's kiss. She felt herself writhe and then press eagerly into his body. She suffered the savaging of disappointment and a sense of loss when he removed his mouth from her own—and then was flung headlong into the sweetness of the pleasure that came when his lips caressed their way along her throat from her ear to her shoulder, and then back along her collarbone. His dark head bent over her, encouraging her to slide her fingers into the heavenly thickness of his hair.

It was like being on a roller coaster.

She could feel her heart thudding so heavily that it seemed to be beating outside her body. And then she realised that the beat she could feel drumming so hard wasn't coming from her own heart but from Falcon's. The sweetest pleasure and triumph pierced her, catching her off guard with its intensity. Falcon was *enjoying* kissing her. Her—a woman who had thought herself not a proper woman at all.

Gratitude and exhilaration filled her, but was quickly forgotten when Falcon kissed her again, taking her mouth and covering it with his own, finding her tongue and teasing it into an erotically intimate dance with his own whilst his hands moved down over her body, his palms just skimming her breasts.

Immediately Annie tensed, her delight in the moment broken by the sharpness of her sudden recognition that things were moving too fast.

As though Falcon himself recognised that fact he released her, leaning his forehead against her own for a second before saying huskily, 'It is just as well this dress of yours does not possess a zip. Because if it did right now I'd be caressing your breasts, learning them with my hands and my lips. There is something almost unbearably erotic about the sight of moonlight on a woman's naked body, caressing it with silver pathways.'

Annie shuddered wildly and pulled back from him.

'I really must go in.'

'Yes,' Falcon agreed meaningfully. 'I think you must—

unless you want me to take this evening's lesson far further than I had originally planned.'

He wasn't really asking her if she wanted what he had just described to her, was he? Annie thought dizzily. He couldn't be. Could he? Her senses swung between fear and excitement. They were a long way from that stage yet, she reassured herself. Indeed, she wasn't even sure she would be able to go that far.

Annie couldn't sleep. She had tried—she had tried very hard. But every time she closed her eyes it was as though she was back in the garden with Falcon. In fact, so vivid were the images conjured up behind her closed eyelids that she could almost feel him, as well as see him. His warmth against her own body, his touch on her skin, his scent, his kiss, his voice sensitising her already over-sensitised mind when he told her what he would do to her.

It was no use. Annie pushed back the covers and slid her feet out of the bed and onto the floor. It was so warm tonight that even the thin cotton tee-shirt-style nightdress she was wearing felt unpleasant and unwanted against her skin. Because what she really wanted was the touch of Falcon's hands?

This was ridiculous. She was glad, of course, that she was rediscovering her sexuality. She just hadn't expected that what she would feel would be so…so intense. She had imagined she would feel nervous and uncertain, too anxious to really enjoy what was happening, but it was as though somehow Falcon had cast some magic spell on her that had cut through those expected feelings.

She walked to the nursery, where Ollie was fast asleep—as she herself should be and no doubt Falcon was.

* * *

Falcon stared unseeingly at the computer screen in front of him. Unable to sleep, he had decided he might as well work on one of his new architectural commissions.

Falcon loved his work. His love of the beauty of Florence's buildings was, he believed, his mother's gift to him, since Florence had been her home. Annie would enjoy Florence, and he would enjoy her pleasure in it. As he had enjoyed her pleasure this evening…

It was no use lying to himself. The truth was that he had been caught off guard by the intensity of his own desire for her—aroused, no doubt, by the sweetness of her response to him.

He sat back in his chair and exhaled slowly. The object of the exercise was not his pleasure but Annie's rediscovery of her lost sexuality. And if he had experienced an arousal and desire with her tonight that he had felt might get out of control then he must ensure that he did not do so again. In future he must experience those things only to the extent that her knowledge of his response would aid her progress. If he could not do that then he would, in his own eyes, be as culpable and as guilty of abusing her as her stepbrother.

He stood up and walked over to the window. His private apartment was in the original part of the *castello*, which he had remodelled sympathetically to create for himself very modern living quarters in what was essentially a twelfth-century building. The walls had been stripped back to their natural stone, where appropriate, and limestone floors had been laid on the ground floor of the two-storey apartment. Damage to the outer wall in one area had allowed him, with modern building techniques, to replace the crumbling wall with a two-storey, floor-to-ceiling glass 'wall', which looked out onto a limestone patio, beyond which an infinity pool melted visually into the sea itself.

Within the area he had renovated there had been enough space to create an inner room, with glass and polished plaster walls, which contained a small modern kitchen again with views towards the sea.

A matt-finish metal staircase led up to a galleried landing and three bedrooms, each with its own bathroom and dressing room area. The apartment was furnished with the very best of modern Italian furniture in natural products like leather and wood, as well as steel and modern textiles, and artwork.

The apartment was a clean open space that breathed light and openness. As an antidote to his father's love of secrecy and control? Falcon frowned. He was digging too deep within himself when there was no need. Better that he thought about Annie than his own childhood.

He doubted that Annie would totally approve of his apartment. She would think it child-unfriendly. Her ideal would no doubt be somewhere more like the villa outside Florence his second brother had bought for his new wife—a large, elegant family home that would happily accommodate any number of children in safety and comfort.

It was his duty, though, as the eldest son to maintain a presence here. When their father died, the people would expect him to be here.

But it was Annie and Oliver and their needs that were preoccupying him right now, rather than those of his people.

Annie. She was invading his thoughts and his senses more deeply and more intensely than he had been prepared for. But that wasn't her fault.

It had been obvious to him that she was devoid of the least idea of how much it had aroused him to feel her body trembling so wildly just because he had caressed her. A reaction like that could go to a man's head far too easily, and could make *her* far too vulnerable.

His body was aching. It had been a long time since he had had a relationship. The effect of too many women throwing themselves at him rather too often and too hard during his twenties had left him picky about the women he dated, and cynical about the likelihood of actually finding love and the right kind of wife in one woman. On a practical level it was important that his wife understood his commitment to his people, and that she was willing to share that commitment with him. But it was equally important to him that his marriage should be one in which husband and wife were faithful to one another. His father's affair had left him with an abhorrence of marital infidelity. His brothers were lucky. They had had the good fortune to fall in love and be loved in return.

He, on the other hand, had to balance his own needs with the needs of the Leopardi name and its people. Passion and practicality. Could they ever go together? Or must one always be sacrificed in order to have the other?

If so, he must favour practicality for the benefit of others over passion for the benefit of himself.

His body still ached with unsatisfied need.

If he closed his eyes it would be all too easy to picture Annie—not as she had been in the garden, but far more intimately, here with him now, clothed only in moonlight, silvering her breasts and dipping shadows between them, turning her nipples as dark as olives, stroking silken pathways along her body. She would taste of night air and warm skin, her breathing shaken by tremors of desire. She would cry out to him as he kissed her and held her. And he would…

He would do nothing other than remember what his role was in her life, Falcon told himself harshly.

'I thought this evening we would concentrate on the small things a man might do to show that he is attracted to a woman.'

They had finished dinner. Ollie was asleep—Annie had been up to check on him—and her nerves were so on edge she was sure that Falcon must notice. It was five days since he had kissed her. Five whole days. And there hadn't been a single one of them when she hadn't relived that kiss over and over again.

'The small things?' Annie repeated. She must not feel disappointed. She must not wish that he would kiss her again. She must *not*!

'Yes,' Falcon confirmed. 'Such as the way a man might hold the gaze of a woman he admires for that little bit longer, looking at her like so.'

His hand under her chin gently turned her face towards his own and slightly upwards, so that his gaze fell directly onto her upturned face and she could see the slow, concentrated way in which he allowed it to almost physically caress her skin.

Tension prickled along her nerve-endings; her heart started to race. She could almost *feel* the heavy weight of his concentration on her mouth. It was impossible for her to stop her lips from parting, and impossible not to look helplessly into his eyes. He was looking at her in a way that made her catch her breath. The blood was pounding in her ears and a mixture of weakness and excitement was pouring through her.

Falcon knew he had to break the spell he himself had

woven, which now trapped him within its sensual mystery. Just looking at Annie's mouth made him want to feel it beneath his own—to feel too the sweetness of her previous response.

This wasn't what he had planned. The object was to encourage her to explore and enjoy her sensuality—not for him to become aroused.

Somehow he managed to drag his gaze away. Although there was nothing he could do about the powerful thumping of his heart.

Annie watched him, torn between disappointment and relief as she saw him win his battle for control.

'I can see how…how erotic something like that could be,' she told him, striving to sound calm and businesslike—after all, what they were doing was a sort of businesslike venture.

'It's amazing, isn't it, that something so…Well, something that's just a look really can have such a powerful effect?' She hesitated, and then told him honestly, 'You make it all seem so natural and…and that it's all right to feel…to want…' She couldn't risk putting into words exactly what he had made her feel, so instead she finished quickly, 'It's not shameful and wrong, like Colin used to say it was.'

'No man worthy of the name would ever make a woman feel ashamed of her sensuality.' Falcon's voice was constricted with the force of his feelings. Her trusting admission had reminded him of the role he had elected to play. His hand dropped away from her face. It might be better in future if he conducted at least some of her lessons in public, where he would surely not be in so much danger from his own reactions.

* * *

'Bring swimming things,' Falcon had said to her yesterday, when he had asked her if she still wanted to see a little more of the island. But it had simply not occurred to Annie that he would bring her and Ollie somewhere as achingly smart and exclusive as this hotel where they had had lunch, after a drive during which Falcon had not only driven at a safe and comfortable speed but had also given her an expert commentary on their surroundings and their architectural past.

She should surely be getting used to the intimacy of being around him now? she told herself. And to all those small touches that came when he pulled out a chair for her, or helped her in any way—the smiles that accompanied the compliments he paid her. All were designed, she knew, to boost her confidence in herself as a woman.

She *was* getting used to them, and she *did* feel comfortable in his presence—but at the same time she also felt confused by the way she herself so often felt. The way she ached inside for him to kiss her again, and her sense of loss when he didn't.

Today, though, they were having a day out with Ollie.

The hotel he had brought them to was close to the town of Taormina, famous for its historical buildings—including the ruins of a Greek theatre—and for its proximity to Mount Etna. Before lunch they had had time to walk down the main street, Falcon insisting on pushing Ollie's buggy, whilst he pointed out various sites of interest to her—including the glamorous Caffè Wunderbar, where Elizabeth Taylor and Richard Burton had sipped cocktails.

Falcon had even told her, leaning closer to her to murmur the words in her ear that, 'D.H. Lawrence holidayed here with his wife.' He had based Mellors the gamekeeper in *Lady Chatterley's Lover* on a boatman from the town, whom Lawrence's wife had seduced. 'Taormina was famous at one time for the effect it had on visiting Englishwomen. You must tell me later if there is any truth in that rumour.'

He had been smiling at her as he spoke, a lazy smile of such intimacy that she had quickly forgotten the small pang of aloneness she had felt earlier, glimpsing a couple ambling along the street totally wrapped up in one another. In fact, having Falcon's concentrated attention fixed on her had made her feel she was in so much danger of becoming dizzy that she had reached out to steady herself, placing her hand on the handle of the buggy, only to have it immediately covered by Falcon's hand closing around it.

It was strange, the effect such small gestures could have. She had wanted to pull her hand away—if only to stop her heart from pounding so heavily—but she had reminded herself that Falcon was trying to teach her what it felt like to experience all those things she should have experienced naturally as she grew from a teenager to a young woman.

Because he'd still had his hand over hers, Falcon had been forced to move closer to her as they'd walked along together, and that had meant that she had been acutely conscious of his thigh brushing hers and of his closeness to her. When they had had to cross a road he had released her hand, but her relief had been short-lived because instead he had placed his arm around her waist, guiding her politely across the road.

'You look terrified,' he had told her once they were safely across. 'This kind of physical intimacy is supposed to be a pleasure. When a man takes every opportunity he can to be close to you, in mundane everyday matters of life and in public, it signifies not just his physical desire for you but also his desire to claim and protect you. If you want his attention then the way to show him would be to lean in a little bit closer to him.' His arm had urged her closer as he had spoken.

'And relax your body so that it moves with his. Then he will probably do something like this.' His hand had moved to the curve of her waist, discreetly caressing it.

Discreet so far as any possible onlookers were concerned. The effect his touch had had on the internal workings of her body had been anything but discreet. Warmth from his hand had spread all over her body, making her breasts grow heavy and her nipples tighten and ache. It had pooled with devastating effect low within her, and her mind had created mental images and physical longings that had made her face burn with self-consciousness.

Was that physical desire? She had felt as though Falcon had unlocked a place within her—the turning of its key unleashing almost frighteningly powerful urges. Like the urge she had experienced during lunch, when Falcon had put his hand on her knee to attract her attention whilst she had been spooning baby food into Ollie's eager mouth, so that he could tell her something. It had been an urge that had meant she would gladly have turned to him in silent invitation for him to slide his hand along the bare length of her thigh.

And he had known what she had been feeling. She was sure of it, Annie thought now, from the shelter of their private tented poolside *cabana* at the same exclusive hotel where they had had lunch.

Annie had seen photographs of such places in the glossy magazines she'd flicked through in doctors' and dentists' waiting rooms, but she'd never expected to experience the reality of one of them for herself.

Their lunch had been served at a private table under the shade of an umbrella, on signature china with heavy designer cutlery, crystal glasses and beautifully laundered linen.

In the baby changing room provided for guests she'd found everything the most fussy and spoiled mother and baby could ever want—although she had noticed that the two other babies in the changing room were accompanied by uniformed nannies and not their mothers.

Now, having changed into her swimsuit whilst Falcon minded Ollie, she was lying in the shade on the most comfortable lounger imaginable, whilst Ollie played happily within her watchful view.

Falcon had gone for a swim—which was perhaps just as well, she admitted, given the effect the constant sight of him clothed in a pair of admittedly perfectly respectable brightly coloured shorts of the type most of the other men also seemed to be wearing had been having on her.

Her swimsuit and its matching prettily embroidered kaftan had been chosen by the personal shopper. Annie hadn't so much as tried them on, convinced that she would never wear *any* of the clothes the shopper had selected, never mind something as revealing as the swimsuit, but she was forced to admit now that it might have been wiser if she had.

In its elegant box the pewter-coloured swimsuit had looked innocuous enough, even a little dull, but once on it had wrapped itself around her curves in a way that, whilst covering her very respectably, had somehow or other managed to create the most sensual of body shapes—and surely a greater length of leg than she really possessed. It had been a relief to slip on the matching pewter kaftan, which thankfully covered her from her throat to her knees.

Now, though, the privacy of the cabana and the relaxing effect of her lunchtime glass of wine had combined to coax her into removing the kaftan and luxuriating in the wonderful warmth of the sun—easily felt despite the shade.

Tired out after his busy day, Ollie was starting to close his eyes. Smiling at her son, Annie got up off her lounger and picked him up, hugging and kissing him before settling him in his buggy for a sleep.

She had just finished tucking Ollie in when Falcon returned to the *cabana* from his swim, the sun catching shoulders surely as broad and powerful as those of any Olympic swimmer, tanned as his whole body was, in a beautiful golden brown. There was something about the close proximity of so much semi-naked masculinity that was making it very difficult for her to breathe, Annie admitted to herself.

Not wanting to be caught by Falcon gazing wide-eyed at his broad shoulders and powerful arms, she let her attention slide lower—only to realise her mistake far too late, when it became trapped in watching drops of water from the pool roll down his chest.

She couldn't breathe properly, couldn't move, couldn't think—but she could certainly feel, and what she was feeling was telling her in no uncertain terms that Falcon had well and truly unleashed her natural instincts. The weight of the water had pulled his shorts low down on his hips, and the sight of the dark arrowing of his body hair was making her feel slightly light headed. Or was it the thudding pound of her heart that was doing that? It didn't matter. All that mattered was her relief when Falcon reached for a towel and started to dry himself.

'I saw you putting sunscreen on Oliver earlier. I hope you've put some on yourself,' he said when he had finished drying his body and was rubbing at his hair.

'Yes. Yes, I have,' Annie told him quickly. She could feel her temperature soaring at the same speed with which her heartbeat was accelerating at the thought of having Falcon offer to perform that task for her.

'Good.' He reached down and picked up the sunscreen she had placed by her sun lounger and handed it to her, requesting, 'Do my back for me, will you?'

What could she say? If she refused he was bound to want to know why—and besides, this was exactly the kind of thing that a woman of her age should be used to doing. Falcon would make allowances for her, she reassured herself as she nodded her head in acquiescence, her throat suddenly too dry for her to be able to trust herself to speak. He knew, after all, that she had no experience of this kind of personal intimacy.

He had presented his back to her now, and was standing with his hands on his hips, waiting.

Her hands were trembling so much she dropped the bottle of lotion, and then struggled to uncap it, causing Falcon to turn round and take it from her, telling her wryly, 'Hold out your hand.' He squeezed a small amount of the lotion into her palm, before turning his back to her a second time.

She started at the back of his neck, suffering the shock of the silky hot feel of his skin against her lotion-slick hands as she worked the cream into his skin as slowly and as carefully as though it had been Ollie's baby skin she was protecting. Beneath her fingertips his shoulders were every bit as strongly muscled as they had looked, and it was hard for her not to give in to the unexpected temptation to trace the shape of his bones with her fingertip. How extraordinary and amazing and life-affirming it was to know that one day her son, her baby, would be like this—a man whom women would admire and desire and love, just as they must Falcon.

Her body stiffened. How many women had there been? How many had he loved back? Why was that sharp pain skewering her heart?

Falcon's voce—'Something wrong?'—brought her back to reality.

'I've run out of lotion,' she told him.

The cap was still off the bottle, but strangely she felt no inclination to point that fact out to him when he picked it up and tipped some more into her waiting hand.

'I'm not Oliver, you know,' he told her. 'In a real man and woman situation there would be nothing wrong and a whole lot right in caressing me as a potential lover whilst you're doing that.'

Immediately Annie stiffened.

'I'm not used to things like this,' she reminded him defensively. It hurt to know that he thought her touch too clinical to be arousing, even though she told herself that it ought not to.

'Perhaps it would be better if I gave you a small demonstration?' Falcon suggested.

Before she could say anything he had poured some of the lotion into his own hand and was turning her around.

She was wearing her hair up in a knot for coolness, and she could feel the warmth of Falcon's breath as he leaned closer to her. Was he going to kiss her? Her stomach turned liquid with a longing that turned to disappointment when he didn't. Only for that disappointment to go up in flames of fresh sensual excitement when he eased the straps of her swimsuit down. Frantically she clutched the front of it to her breasts, whilst Falcon began to slowly stroke and circle trails of hot desire on the vulnerable flesh of her bare back.

How could something as simple as putting on sun cream be so unbearably erotic? Annie felt as though she had entered a whole new world of sensation and discovery. What Falcon was doing was giving her a master class in the art of sensual massage, she recognized, as her body took fire and her inhibitions were burned away.

Long before he had reached the base of her spine her body was urging her to beg him to remove her swimsuit completely and take her in his arms. Surely it wasn't possible for her to be feeling like this so quickly, so easily, and so…so intensely? Perhaps Colin had been right when he had warned her all those years ago that there was something about her that meant she needed protecting from her own too-sexual nature?

As though somehow her thoughts and fears had communicated themselves to Falcon, he turned her around to face him, his hands firm and cool on her upper arms, holding her safe, making her *feel* safe.

'You are aroused and that is exactly what I intended to happen,' he told her calmly. 'It's a completely natural reaction to my deliberately erotic stimulation of your body and your senses. It's nothing to feel ashamed of or concerned about. Rather, you should feel proud of your inbuilt ability to be the woman nature designed you to be. No matter what your stepbrother might have told you, responding sensually to a man who has aroused your desire does not make you bad or promiscuous or any of the other things I suspect he said to poison you against yourself.'

'Thank you for saying that.' Annie could feel tears threatening to sting her eyes. 'I was questioning how… how appropriate it was for me to feel what…what I was feeling so quickly and so—so very *much*.'

'It was entirely appropriate. And, if it makes you feel happier, I have to confess that I was equally aroused myself.'

Annie looked at him uncertainly before venturing to ask, 'Is that good or bad?'

'It's both good *and* bad,' Falcon answered enigmatically, slanting her one of those sidelong looks of assessment that made her bones melt and her pulse race. She had used up more than her allowance of courage for one day. She couldn't bring herself to ask him just what his response meant.

'Now,' Falcon announced briskly, handing her the lotion, 'it's your turn to practise on me what I have just shown you.'

'You mean, you want me to make *you* feel the way you just made *me* feel?' The words were out before she could call them back, leaving her feeling wretchedly gauche and foolish, but Falcon seemed not to notice, simply nodding his head and agreeing.

'I certainly want you to try. I promise you that when you do meet a man with whom you want to have sex you will want not just to arouse him with your touch but to touch him simply for the pleasure it will give you. And you will feel much more confident doing so if you know what you are doing.'

She knew that he was right. But even so she could feel herself baulking at what he had told her he wanted her to do.

There was no point in arguing, though. Falcon had already stretched himself out full-length on his front on one of the loungers, his head pillowed on his forearms.

Annie tried not to feel alarmed, but to think instead of what she was doing as a practical exercise. Falcon had started at the back of her neck, causing delicious little thrills of pleasure to course through her and then to cascade down her body as he worked his way down it. She must try to mirror his movements.

She felt awkward at first, not sure how to touch him or where, simply copying what he had done to her. But within a very short space of time her own pleasure—the pleasure she was deriving from touching him—took over, totally obliterating her earlier self-consciousness.

When she heard Falcon exhale sharply as she stroked her fingertips down his spine, a thrill of triumph shot through her, emboldening her to slowly caress the taut flesh ether side of the base of his spine, using both hands as she moved out towards his hips, loving the feel of male flesh and muscle and bone beneath her touch.

In fact, such was her pleasure in what she was doing that at one point she leaned forward and pressed her lips to his skin, hesitantly at first, and then with more confidence as she heard the sound that escaped from his lungs—more of a slight groan than a mere breath, its pent-up sexual tension increasing the ache in her own lower body. If he'd been wearing briefer swimming shorts, or even just a towel, she'd have been able to move lower, to stroke the dark haired breadth of his powerful thighs.

That part of her that contained the mystery and the mechanics of the female orgasm quivered and fluttered and then ached into a pulsing life that froze her into complete shock—just at the same time as Falcon turned over and reached for her, lifting her with one easy movement from her position kneeling beside the lounger to lie against his body.

Like sheet lightning the most exquisite pleasure burst through her in an almost unbearable ache of delight that had her both appalled by her own runaway reaction to him, wanting to pull back, and yet so eager for more that she desperately wanted to press herself closer to him.

His lips were close to her ear, and when he murmured in it, 'Very good…' fresh quivers of arousal hurled themselves through her body. 'But one word of warning. When you do this for real, it might be better to ascertain how strong your partner's self-control is before you start. Especially if you are in a public place. Because right now you have aroused me to a very improper state for where we are, and I have to award you full marks and the continuation of your lesson this evening in my apartment.'

Did his words mean what she thought they meant? That tonight he would take things to their natural conclusion? She wanted to protest, to tell him that things were moving too fast and that she wasn't ready, but his hand was over her heart, measuring its frantic beat. How could she deny that was what she wanted when her own heartbeat was giving her away and telling him the truth?

Fortunately she had a cast iron excuse to delay things.

'I can't leave Ollie,' she told him truthfully. Her son was her first concern at all times and in all ways.

'You won't need to leave him. You can bring him with you. I'm sure that he won't mind sleeping in a travel cot for once. I asked Maria to make sure that she ordered one just in case you ever wanted to accompany me to Florence.'

The gate was closed, the die cast, the decision made. Tonight she would lie naked in Falcon's arms in Falcon's bed, and he would teach her body all that it needed to know to be free. She had to say something.

She half stumbled into speech. 'You love Florence, don't you?' It was an attempt to cling on to some edge of social normality—a difficult task when she was lying half naked on top of him and his arm was holding her firmly against his body.

'Yes.' Falcon reached for her hand, closing her fingers over her palm and looking down at it as though he wanted to guard his words and his emotions. 'Which is why my father was probably right to claim when I was a child that I was not enough of a Leopardi to succeed him—that I was more my mother's child than his. Unfortunately for him, and for me, I am his eldest son. Therefore, no matter how much he would have liked to put Antonio in my place, nothing short of my death and the deaths of both my brothers could have achieved that. As a boy I used to fear that—'

He broke off, but Annie guessed what he had been about to say. 'You were afraid that your father might try to harm you?'

'I was afraid for my brothers,' he admitted.

His hand was still curled round her palm, and without thinking she placed her other hand on top of it in a gesture of silent comfort.

'That must have been dreadful for you.' She could easily imagine how dreadful. He had such a strongly developed sense of duty and responsibility towards others that it was only natural that as the eldest he should have felt protective of his brothers even if their family life had been a happy one. But when she added the burden of the tensions and fears he had just admitted to, it filled Annie with a protective surge of almost maternal emotion to think of what Falcon the boy had had to endure.

'My father would never have hurt them—or me, of course. He spoke merely out of the frustration of his excessive love for Antonio. It is not without irony, though, he felt that the son he did lose should have been his favourite. It is my opinion that the responsibility for Antonio's faults of character can be placed at our father's door. He spoiled and indulged Antonio from the moment of his birth—and, worse, taught and encouraged him to copy his own attitude of contempt towards the three of us. He allowed Antonio to grow up believing he was invincible, beyond any form of law or retribution. He was in many ways the orchestrator and the cause of Antonio's death, and it is my belief that he knows that.'

'Sometimes I worry that Ollie might have inherited some of Antonio's…failings,' Annie admitted, putting into words for the first time a fear that haunted the deepest recesses of her own heart.

'Oliver is himself,' Falcon assured her, immediately and with firm authority. 'He has you to love and protect him, and if you will allow me, until such time as you do find a man with whom you wish to share your life and bear more children, I would like to stand as his protector and the male influence in his life. You need not fear that my love for him will be tainted by his relationship to Antonio. He is a child of my blood—Leopardi blood—and that is all that matters to me. He will have my love for as long as I am alive to give it to him.'

Tears filled Annie's eyes. She had never imagined that

a man as male as Falcon could speak like this, and be so in accord with her own emotions.

'My father had hoped to discover a grandson that he could mould in his lost son's image. But I am not a boy any longer, I am a man, and I will not allow him to ruin Oliver as he did Antonio.'

Annie moved imperceptibly closer to him, alarmed by the thought of the Prince trying to control her precious son.

'Maria told me that you are not expecting your father to live very much longer.'

'We were warned that he would not have much more time, but the new medication he is on seems to have give him a fresh lease of life. Despite all the pain he has caused us, I know that neither I or my brothers want his death.'

'No, of course not,' Annie agreed instantly.

Her hand still rested comfortingly on Falcon's. He looked up at her, and then said softly, 'I was right about you. You are a very seductive woman.'

Annie looked down at their hands.

'No, not that,' Falcon told her. 'It is your compassion and your tenderness that make you seductive—not just the passion you keep so firmly hidden away. But tonight we shall see it revealed as its own fiercely sweet self.'

Annie could feel herself starting to tremble. She didn't resist when Falcon released her hand and then lifted his own newly free hand to the back of her head, so that he could pull her down towards him to kiss her.

It was only the briefest of kisses—just the mere brush of his lips against hers—but it was enough to tell her just how eagerly her body would respond to him later.

CHAPTER EIGHT

ANNIE had had a full tour of Falcon's apartment, and was genuinely impressed, and filled with admiration for everything about it—especially the double-height floor-to-ceiling glass wall of the living room and the master bedroom.

'There are no curtains,' she had commented in surprise. She had noticed this lack as she and Falcon had stood side by side, looking out across the clifftop to the sea beyond. Falcon had insisted on holding Ollie, who had been grizzling a little bit—preparatory, Annie thought, to cutting a new tooth. He had smiled widely with delight the minute Falcon had taken him in his arms.

'No, this corner of the *castello*, very private,' Falcon had agreed. 'I like the freedom of lying in bed and watching the night sky—just as I like the freedom of being able to walk naked around my own personal space, and swim naked in my pool. They are simple pleasures, but very meaningful to those who cherish them. There is nothing to compare with the cloak of the night sky on one's naked body, like the touch of velvet, or the silken brush of water against bare skin.'

'I wouldn't know,' Annie had told him, uncomfortably aware of just what the images his words were drawing inside her head were doing to her body.

'Well, tonight you can know, if you wish,' he had said softly. Which had had her running for the safety of banal conversation rather than the bold acceptance of his offer which her body had demanded.

To her astonishment Falcon had cooked their dinner himself—a delicious fresh fish dish, served with stuffed vegetables and pasta in a delicately textured sauce, although he had freely admitted the chef had prepared it for him earlier.

'What will the staff think about me having dinner alone here with you?' she had asked, a little apprehensively.

His answer had been a dismissive, confident shrug.

'They will think that I have invited you to have dinner with me in my private quarters. Nothing more—nothing less.'

Did that mean that he regularly entertained women here? she had wondered. And had then had to question just why she had felt such a savage surge of emotion at that thought.

Now she had put Ollie to bed in his travel cot in the dressing room off Falcon's bedroom, so that she would hear him if he woke up. She knew that Falcon would be waiting for her to continue what they had started earlier, but inexplicably—or perhaps sensibly she didn't know—she felt self-consciously reluctant to go to him. But, having come this far, she must do so—there could be no going back. Not if she wanted to be the mother Ollie deserved to have.

Taking a deep breath, she opened the dressing room door and stepped into the bedroom—which was empty.

Confused, she looked uncertainly around the room—and then tensed as Falcon emerged from the bathroom, wearing a robe.

'I'm going to have a swim. Why don't you join me?'

Did he mean a naked swim? Was he wearing anything under that robe?

Her heart was thudding, and that fluttering, pulsing wanton aching that she had felt earlier had started up again.

'I'd better stay here in case Ollie wakes up,' she answered feebly.

A staircase led down from the bedroom to the patio and pool area below, and Annie vowed that she would *not* watch Falcon to see whether or not he was planning to swim in the nude. Instead she determinedly went back down the stairs to retrieve the white wine spritzer she had abandoned earlier, when she had come to put Ollie to bed.

Music was playing softly in the background of the living room, but it was impossible for her to relax. She went back upstairs, to be nearer to Ollie, and moved anxiously round the room, drinking her spritzer and determinedly not looking in the direction of the pool. Which was no doubt why she was taken completely off guard when Falcon came up behind her, relieved her of her almost empty glass and turned her into his arms.

'Now, where were we?' he said firmly, before he silenced her surprised gasp with the hard warmth of his mouth on hers.

He had kissed her before—more than once—so she should have known what to expect. And of course she did. But this time the effect of his kiss on her was magnified a hundred times—no, a thousand, she thought headily as his teeth tugged sensually at her bottom lip so that his tongue could run inside its softness. Then, when she was aching for it to plunge deeper, he withdrew to place tiny, nibbling kisses at the corners of her mouth and tease the pleading parted longing of her lips with the slow, deliberate caress of his tongue.

Annie had no idea just when she had stood up on her tiptoes and pressed herself fiercely against him, her fingers digging into his arms, and then wrapped her arms around his neck to hold him as close to her as she could, whilst her frustrated senses tried to show him what she wanted in place of his teasing caress that was leaving her so hungry and so unsatisfied.

Somewhere at some deep level she knew she must have recorded his encouraging words.

'Yes, that's it—show me that you want me.' He had murmured them in her ear after disengaging his mouth from hers for a thankfully brief few seconds, before returning to reward her for her willingness as a pupil with the slow, soft pressure of his mouth on hers, speedily upgrading the intense and intimate meeting of lips and tongues she had longed for, leaving her to hunger for even greater intimacy.

Miraculously, as though somehow he knew of her desire, he stroked his tongue deep into her mouth, its thrusts long and slow, making her go soft and boneless, as though she was already accommodating him within her, her muscles closing eagerly around him.

Beyond the window the patio and the pool, which had been floodlit whilst Falcon had swum, were now almost in darkness. The only light was that supplied by the stars and the fattening curve of the moon as they sent trails of silver glinting and dancing on both the sea and the pool. That same light was coming through the vast expanse of glass window, turning their surroundings into monochrome mystery highlighted with silver, so that the shadows of the bedroom seemed alluring and enticing, something that belonged to another world—a world of fiction and fantasy into which she could safely step, leaving the harshness of reality unwanted and outside the special empowering sensuality of the here and now.

Or at least that was as close as she was going to allow herself to get to rationalising or analysing her sudden sense of freedom to do and be what she most wanted, stroked into her senses with each passionate thrust of Falcon's tongue against her own. It certainly had to be the reason she was as happy to shed her dress as though it were an unwanted skin she was sloughing off, leaving her wantonly free to be caressed by the night and the look that Falcon was giving her.

His soft words, 'Perfect—you are as perfect as I knew you would be,' Made her eye him boldly, longing to replicate his easy removal of her clothes so that she could repay the compliment. Her stomach muscles tensed with fierce excitement. She didn't need Falcon to remove his bathrobe for her to know that he would be total male perfection. After all, she had already seen most of him that afternoon. Most of him, but not all of him….

Wasn't that exactly the kind of thought Colin had warned her against? For a second Annie hovered between past and present, her old teenage fear chilling through her veins. But again, as though he knew what she was thinking, Falcon drew her towards him and wrapped her in his arms, murmuring against her ear.

'This is where what we started this afternoon ends and where what we both really wanted then begins.'

He was kissing the hollow behind her ear, trailing his fingertips down the side of her neck and then along her shoulder to her arm, kissing his way towards her mouth.

She was aware of him and of her own physical arousal with every single cell in her body. There wasn't a particle of her that wasn't affected by his touch and responsive to it. She wasn't wearing a bra—it hadn't been necessary as her dress had its own built in support—and now the only support her breasts wanted was his hands cupping them whilst he kissed her and brought her tight nipples to even harder aching longing with the pads of his thumbs and the erotic pluck of his finger and thumb. That aroused such a firestorm of sensation within her that she was forced to cry out against it, feeling scarcely able to bear its intensity.

In response Falcon moved back towards the bed, drawing her with him as he sat down on the mattress, pulling her between his open legs and holding her there whilst he circled first one of her nipples and then the other with his tongue-tip, gently at first, so that the torment of her pleasure had her straining towards him, and then more fiercely, lapping at the stiff, swollen, moon-silvered flesh.

Her head thrown back, her spine arched, Annie was lost—a helpless prisoner to her own desire. She felt Falcon's arm supporting her, a sure, strong iron band against her lower back, holding her safe whilst he drew spirals of hot liquid longing on her taut belly with the fingers of his free hand, dipping lower to the barrier of her brief silky knickers, wet now with the excretions of her fierce desire, an unwanted restriction.

Falcon stroked the swollen mound of her sex through the fragile fabric—a light touch that sent Annie wild and made her long for something more intense, more intimate.

His lips opened over one of her nipples, his tongue probing and stroking, and then his teeth gently grating against her hot flesh. At the same time he slid his hand into the leg of her briefs and probed the fullness of the lips covering her sex.

Annie never even heard herself cry out—the sharp, high and wild woman's cry of aching unbearable need—but Falcon did.

Somewhere in the deepest recesses of his conscious he knew that his own arousal—his own need for this woman—was out of control. But for once he wasn't willing to listen to his own inner voice of warning. Annie's arousal, her complete and total offering of herself and her desire to him, in mute acceptance of her trust that he could and would satisfy it and her, overwhelmed him.

He wanted to know her completely—to take her and fill her with the result of his own desire for her. He wanted to hear her cries of orgasm. He wanted to touch and pleasure all of her, with his hands, with his lips, with words and in silence, until she was completely, totally and only his.

He slid down her briefs, breathing in the sweet, musky woman scent of her and feeling his whole body surge on a tsunami of arousal. He slid to the floor, still holding her, his hands spread wide against her rounded cheeks, kneading them erotically as he kissed the inside of her thigh.

Annie was lost, totally and completely, inhabiting a world she had never thought she would know—a world in which just the sensation of another's breath against her skin was enough to have the ache inside her threatening to burst out of control. The slow caress of Falcon's lips and tongue on the inside of her thigh was making her protest volubly against the growing pressure of her own need as she tried to hold it inside her.

It was too late though. It was the final unbearable pressure, Falcon's throaty words—'This is what I wanted to do this afternoon.' He sprang the dam of her desire, resulting in the convulsive contraction of her body into a flood of sensation she was totally unable to withstand.

So this was an orgasm—this was what she had been denying herself during all these years when she had woken from her sleep, aching, somehow knowing what was waiting for her but feeling too afraid to do anything about it because of Colin. Now Falcon had shown her what her own pleasure was.

He was scooping her up in his arms, her body limp with release and satisfaction, and her lips curved into a smile as she put them to his ear and whispered, 'Thank you.'

His skin tasted warm, tempting her to nuzzle deeper into it and then wrap her arms around his neck whilst she burrowed closer to him, driven by an instinct she was too relaxed to question to be close to him, to prolong their intimacy.

He should send her back to her own room. Things had progressed far enough for now. He might be aching with unsatisfied arousal, but the purpose of the exercise was not to satisfy *his* desire.

But she'd never make it back to her room under her own steam. She was practically falling asleep in his arms now, and he was damned if he was going to carry her naked all the way there when there was a perfectly good bed here, Falcon told himself. He pulled back the bedclothes and placed Annie on the bed, covering her up before going to check on Oliver.

The baby was contentedly asleep, twin fans of dark lashes lying on his cheeks concealing eyes that were a direct copy of his own. Falcon stood looking down at him for several seconds, mentally deriding himself for the fierce tug this small human being had on his emotions. Oliver wasn't even his child, and yet he felt as protective of him as though he had created him himself.

This child must not be damaged and spoiled by his father as Antonio had been. And the best way to ensure that that did not happen was for Annie to find a partner who would protect and rear Oliver as though he were his own. Something deep within Falcon felt as though it was being wrenched apart, causing a fierce stab of angry, denying pain to thrust through him.

What was the matter with him? That was, after all, in part the purpose of this evening's intimacy, wasn't it? That Annie should have the confidence to find herself a man?

It was because Oliver was a Leopardi that he was feeling the way he was. Because it was bred into his bones that Leopardi children—especially Leopardi children without their natural fathers—should be brought up here in Sicily, knowing their heritage.

He was getting as bad as his father, Falcon derided himself.

His body still ached fiercely with unsatisfied desire. He should go for another swim to rid himself of it. But instead for some reason, when he walked back into the bedroom, what he did was shrug off his bathrobe and slide into the bed next to Annie, drawing her sleeping body into his arms.

CHAPTER NINE

'IT IS so lovely having you and Ollie living here, Annie. Sometimes I have to pinch myself in case I'm dreaming. I feel I've been so lucky.'

Annie nodded her head and tried to look as though she was paying proper attention to what Julie was saying as the two of them sat drinking tea and watching their babies playing happily together on the shaded patio of Rocco's beautiful mansion. The reality, though, was that she was finding it next to impossible to drag her thoughts away from the intoxicating and guilty pleasure of reliving over and over again the events of two nights ago, when she had woken up in the velvet darkness to find herself in bed with Falcon.

Still buoyed up with the sweet physical satisfaction of her earlier orgasm, and the emotional high of feeling that she had finally broken free of her imprisonment and celebrated her sexuality, she had been filled with unfamiliar confidence and happiness.

It was those feelings, she felt sure, that had somehow led to her not only stretching luxuriously against Falcon, savouring the sensuality of being in her own skin and at one with her sensuality, but also being proactive enough to decide that the rush of pleasure it gave her to stretch out and feel Falcon's skin against her own was a pleasure that needed further exploration.

From that thought it had only been the merest heartbeat of a step—the simple raising of her hand to place it palm-down flat against Falcon's chest so that she could absorb the simple but delightful pleasure of feeling his heart beat against her touch—to discovering the temptation to do far more than that.

The fact that Falcon had been asleep wasn't something that had even registered with her. She had been on such a high of thrilling confidence and sensual joy. Her new sense of freedom had swept away all normal rationality. She had been lost, totally and utterly, in a daze of such sensual delight and arousal, so pleased with herself for being able to feel that way, that she simply hadn't been able to stop herself from letting her new-found womanhood have its way.

She had stroked her fingertips along Falcon's bare arm, kissed her way from the place where her head had rested on his chest close to his heart right up to his throat—spending endless absorbed and entranced minutes, or so it had seemed, exploring the hollow at the base of his throat with her tongue-tip, painting swirls of delighted gratitude there for all that he had given her. And then, when the languorous, relaxed happiness she had been feeling started to transform into an aroused ache, she'd continued to stroke her tongue over his Adams's apple and then upwards, diverting towards his ear, leaning across him as she did so. Every movement of her lips had seemed to necessitate a similar movement of her already tight breasts against his chest, the friction caused by the movement of her still-sensitised nipples against his body hair rekindling a powerful surge of the need she had experienced earlier in the evening.

Quite how or when her hand had drifted down to his hip, her fingertips itching to stroke lower, she had no idea. All she did know was that even now, nearly two full days later, just recalling the moment when Falcon had moved, turned his head and murmured in her ear, 'Either you stop right now, or you accept the consequences of what you are doing,' brought back a tumultuously intense echo of what she had felt then, accompanied by an all too familiar dragging ache low down in her body.

Of course she should have stopped. She had found her sensuality, after all, so there had been no real need at all, absolutely none, for Falcon to continue with his teaching programme. But she hadn't stopped. Wild horses, if available, would not have had the least impact on her desire *not* to stop. And not only had she not stopped, she had deliberately moved her hand lower, stroking her fingers through the thick, slightly damp heat of the hair above it until she had reached Falcon's firm erection.

How a woman who had had no knowledge of the intimacy of a man's body could have known such a fiercely possessive female desire to caress and control such maleness she had no idea. All she knew was that she had done so.

Falcon had suffered her caressing exploration for a handful of heat-charged minutes, during which her heartbeat had raced to match the thunder of his and the air between them had become filled with the heightened sound of their mutually unsteady breathing. His flesh, already firm beneath her fingertips, had grown harder and wider. And then he had groaned out loud—a raw, guttural, utterly visceral sound that had thrilled through her, reaching deep into her body to turn its already aroused flutter into a driving, urgent pulse. Then he had reached for her, pulling her down on top of his own body, his hands pressing her hips down against his hardness and then sweeping possessively up over her back and into her hair whilst he held her against his mouth and kissed the breath out of her.

He had broken his kiss only to tell her in a semi-tortured, throaty voice, 'I want you. I want you right here, right now.'

'I want you too,' she had whispered back.

She had been the one to tug urgently on his hands, shivering with raw delight when he had rolled her beneath him. The moonlight had been a silver, sweat-slick pathway over his skin, revealing to her the male desire burning in his gaze, its intensity mirroring the dangerous heat licking at her own nerve endings.

She'd had a child, rejoiced in his birth, unconcerned then about the effect that physical experience might have on her body. But suddenly she had been acutely aware of how much that process might have changed her. And not just that process. She might have no memory of what had happened with Antonio, but it had happened.

Somewhere deep down in her most secret self she had felt a pang of something primitive she hadn't really wanted to admit to: a mixture of longing and grief and recognition of the fact that Falcon was the man, the lover, was, given the choice, she would have wanted to be her first.

He had kissed her face and then her throat, moving over her, touching her sex with his fingers as he had done before. This time the rush of sensation that had filled her was stronger and deeper, arching her up towards him.

He'd kissed her breasts and then asked softly, 'Are you sure you want this?'

She had, she remembered, laughed a little unsteadily before telling him truthfully, 'Yes—and a thousand times more than I have ever imagined I could want it.'

In the moonlight she had seen his chest expand and then contract.

'I'll need to take precautions,' he had told her. 'I won't be a second.'

She had known that what he was saying made sense, but suddenly the thought of him leaving her was one she hadn't been able to bear. She had clung to him, wrapping her arms tightly around him, pressing her pelvis into him with aching need as she had told him, 'No.'

Would he have stayed if she hadn't rubbed herself against him so provocatively, her body convulsing in open and delirious pleasure and need as she'd felt his hardness against her sex? She didn't know. What she did know was that the pleasure of her own wanton sensuality had been so intense that she had repeated the movement—not once, but several times.

His control had broken then, and he had positioned her, lifting her slightly so that he could thrust slowly and deliberately into her.

'If you want me to stop—' he had begun, but she had shaken her head, showing him rather than telling him how little she wanted that by wrapping her legs around him and rising up to meet his thrust.

After that the world had become a whirligig of different pleasures, each one more intense than the last. A kaleidoscope of shared need and movement. Her flesh had clasped itself greedily around him as each thrust took him deeper into her, taking her higher and higher.

Having him inside her had felt so right—like nothing

she could ever have imagined. He had filled her and completed her, and the pleasure had grown and kept on growing, leaving her so lost in the marvel of it that her orgasm had caught her unawares, overwhelming her so swiftly that she'd wanted to hold it back so that she could enjoy the sensation for longer.

The echoes of it had still been shuddering through her when Falcon had arched and tensed before thrusting one last time, the agonised joy of his male triumph reverberating through the silver night.

She had cried a little afterwards, for no good reason at all, and if that hadn't been shameful enough she had then compounded her silliness by telling Falcon emotionally, 'That was wonderful. I just wish that you had been the first.'

The first, the last and the only.

Ollie's protesting wail as he and Josh reached for the same toy brought her abruptly back to reality.

'When is Falcon due back from Florence?' Julie was asking her.

'Not until tomorrow evening some time.'

She saw the look that Julie gave her and tried not to blush. Her words had betrayed all too clearly that she was missing Falcon and wanted his return.

She'd only learned that he'd left the *castello* and gone to Florence when Maria had told her. Annie had returned to her own room to sleep, of course. After all, she and Falcon weren't a couple in the normal sense. But her bed had seemed empty and cold after the warmth of his and his presence in it. The whole *castello* felt empty and cold without him, in fact.

Like the rest of her life would be without him?

Annie jumped as though she'd touched something that had given her a small electric shock. What kind of silly thinking was that? How could her life be empty when she had a son and now, thanks to Falcon, the ability to find herself a proper partner and to make a commitment to that partner? But the only man she wanted to make a commitment to and with was Falcon.

No! She must not think like that. She could not and would not. Having her fall in love with him had most certainly not been the purpose of Falcon's plan to help her recover her repressed sexuality. He would be horrified if he were ever to discover how she felt. It had to remain her secret.

'I worry about the Prince when Falcon isn't here,' she said, excusing her reaction to Julie. 'Especially after your warning to me.'

It was the truth in one sense. She had felt distinctly anxious earlier in the day, when Maria had told her that the Prince's manservant had said that his master wanted to see 'the child', and that he—the manservant—would come and collect Ollie, to take him to see his grandfather. Her presence was not required.

It was silly to feel so afraid and vulnerable because Falcon wasn't there. After all what could his father do? He was a frail elderly man, and Ollie was *her* son.

Falcon pushed to one side the plans he had been studying. It was no use. He was only deceiving himself if he thought he was actually going to do any work. There had only been one place his thoughts had been since the evening Annie had shared his bed, and that had been with her.

Falcon had always considered his attitude—no, he corrected himself harshly, he had *prided* himself on his attitude to others and their needs, but now he recognised that he had been guilty of hubris. In his arrogance and his inability to recognise his own human vulnerability he had not seen the danger of what he was planning to do—for himself and, even more unforgivably, for Annie.

There was no point telling himself that his motives had been altruistic, based on a genuine belief that he had a duty to help her. He should have known and factored in the risk of his own weakness. He was human, after all. Very human—as the evening he had spent in bed with Annie had proved.

He had believed that he was doing the right thing, and that there was no risk to either of them. No risk? When he had broken the golden rule of modern sexual relationships by not using a condom? How much more evidence of his own reckless risk taking did he need to be confronted with before he admitted his fallibility and his error?

He had challenged fate, thoughtlessly and arrogantly, and now he was having to pay the price. But worse than that, with his behaviour he had broken the bond of trust he had assured Annie she could depend on. The plain, unvarnished truth was, as he had now been forced to concede, that he had wanted her from the minute he had first held her. Something had been communicated then, from the feel of her in his arms, that had seeded itself directly into his senses—and his heart. Wilfully he had ignored all the warning signs along the way, and deliberately he had encouraged her to believe that he would be her saviour.

Her saviour! He was no better than Antonio in what he had done, even if in his arms she had learned and discovered true sexual pleasure. Just as in hers *he* had learned and discovered what it was to love?

A shudder ran through his body, causing him to push back from his desk and stand up. From the window of his office in his Florence apartment, in the beautiful eighteenth-century *palazzo* that had come down to him through his mother's family, Falcon looked down into the elegant courtyard garden.

He had stolen from Annie, abused her just as surely as his half-brother had done—even if Annie herself was not aware of that as yet; even if before she had finally fallen asleep in his arms she had whispered to him her joyful thanks for what they had shared.

Somewhere, somehow, during their intimacy, a line had been crossed that he had had no right to allow her to cross. He owed her an apology and an explanation. The former he could and would give her, but as for the latter…

What would he explain? That he had concealed the truth from himself and thus by default from her when he had not admitted to himself that his actions were in part motivated by his own desire for her? That admission should have been made, and with it a choice given to her. He had not been honest either with her or with himself, and Annie would have every right to treat him with anger and contempt. Those were certainly the emotions he felt towards himself. And was he really sure that his motivating need right now to be with her stemmed from a desire to admit his failings to her? Was he really sure that the reason he wanted to be with her wasn't that he wanted to repeat the intimacy they had already shared?

What he had done was, in his own eyes, a gross violation of all that he believed his duty to Annie to be.

He had seen his brothers fall in love and find their love was returned, and he had envied them their happiness. Now he envied them even more.

Because he was falling in love with Annie?

He could not, must not, *would* not do that. He had after all promised her the freedom to make her own choice. He must never burden her with his feelings. From now on they must be his secret and his alone.

He had a dinner engagement here in Florence tonight, with a fellow architect and his wife.

But there was only one place he wanted to be right now, and one person he wanted to be with.

CHAPTER TEN

THEY were within sight of the *castello* when a taxi coming away from it passed them on the road, causing Annie to feel a fierce spiral of joyous anticipation, and the hope that it meant that Falcon had returned earlier than planned.

But after Rocco's driver had dropped her off, she asked Maria if Falcon was back, and the housekeeper shook her head and said that no, the taxi had brought a visitor—the second that afternoon—for the Prince. She grumbled that she suspected Falcon knew nothing of these two visits, and that she hoped that two visitors in one day would not be too much for the elderly man.

Nodding her head, Annie was more concerned about the danger of her disappointed reaction to the fact that the taxi had *not* brought Falcon back to the *castello*, than curious about the Prince's visitors.

Now, having fed and changed Ollie, she was walking round the enclosed courtyard garden adjacent to the terrace with him. He lay back in his buggy enjoying the warmth of the late-afternoon sunshine.

She was totally oblivious, until she happened to catch sight of her own reflection in the tranquil goldfish pond beside which she had stopped, of just how accustomed she had become to her new clothes, and how relaxed she now felt about the way they subtly enhanced her womanliness. It was a sweet moment of true female pleasure and one that made her smile.

She had Falcon to thank for that, of course. He had given her the confidence to accept that only *she* had the right to decide what she would wear, and to believe that she was perfectly capable of deciding for herself what was and what was not appropriate. Her skin had begun to develop a light tan, and her hair was loose on her shoulders. She lifted Ollie out of his buggy and, holding him securely showed him the goldfish pond, sitting down at the side of it with him on her lap and disturbing the smooth surface of the water so that he could see the fat goldfish swimming off. This was an idyllic place for him to grow up. He would have the company of Rocco and Julie's little boy, and no doubt there would be other children to come. He would be surrounded by love, and best of all he would have Falcon to guide and protect him.

Falcon. She let her lips form his name, savouring the luxury of the heady pleasure of doing so, knowing that he wasn't here to witness and object to her folly.

The evening stretched out ahead of her, lonely and empty without Falcon's company, just like the previous two evenings had been. She missed him so much. It made no difference that she had known him for such a short space of time. How much time did it take to fall in love? No time at all. A mere heartbeat was enough to change the whole course of a person's life. And Falcon had done that for her. She already owed him so much. She must not add another burden to those she had already given him. Motivated as he was by duty, and his sense of responsibility toward others, no doubt if he found out she loved him he would be concerned on her behalf.

She could see Maria coming towards her through the garden, no doubt to ask her what she wanted for dinner, Annie decided.

But when Maria reached her she announced breathlessly, 'The Prince wishes to see you and Oliver in his apartment.'

'What? Now?' Annie questioned the housekeeper uncertainly.

'Yes. Now.'

He asked for me too?

Previously it had been Falcon who had taken her son to see his grandfather, the Prince having shown no interest in her after their initial meeting.

'You must hurry,' Maria told her, looking anxious. 'The Prince does not like to be kept waiting.'

Ideally, Annie would have preferred to be given an opportunity to freshen up—to make sure that both she and Ollie, especially Ollie, were looking their best before they were subjected to what she suspected would be a very critical inspection by the Prince. But Maria was making it very plain that there would be no time for that kind of luxury.

Indeed, the housekeeper had put out her hand to the buggy, quite obviously wanting to hurry them along.

There was nothing Annie could do other than go along with what was happening, and she wheeled Ollie in his buggy over the immaculately polished floors and priceless antique carpets of the *castello*'s succession of formal reception rooms until they reached the discreetly tucked away lift that went up to the Prince's private apartments on the first floor.

Maria went up in the lift with them, and once it had stopped and the doors had opened handed them over to the manservant who was waiting for them.

The old Prince was a stickler for tradition, Annie had learned from Julie, and lived very much in the style of the early nineteen-hundreds, waited on by a formidable retinue of equally elderly retainers.

This part of the *castello* felt and looked very different from Falcon's modern apartments. The decor of the two empty salons she was almost marched through was very baroque—the ceilings intricately plastered, gilded like the heavily carved woodwork, the wall panels hung with silks that matched those used for the curtains and the soft furnishings. These rooms felt more like a museum than a home, Annie reflected, shivering a little in her sleeveless sundress.

A liveried footman stood on guard outside the final pair of double doors which he and Annie's escort drew back, so that she could enter the room beyond.

Here, if anything, the decor was even more imposing than it had been in the two previous salons. Huge paintings in sombre colours dominated the walls, whilst over her head the ceiling fresco could, she thought, have rivalled the Sistine chapel.

The heavy velvet curtains either side of the room's four windows shut out almost all the natural daylight, so that the room was ablaze with chandeliers, whilst a fire burned in the enormous fireplace.

The air smelled of old age—both human and non-human—but Annie no longer had the luxury of assessing her surroundings. She was unable to drag her shocked, disbelieving gaze from one of the two dark-suited men stand-

ing beside the shrunken figure of the Prince, wrapped in a
rug and seated in his wheelchair beside the fire.

Colin! What was he doing here?

Her heart started to jolt sickeningly inside her chest,
thudding with familiar fear, and she began to shiver and
then tremble as her stepbrother's familiar disapproving
gaze focused on her bare shoulders and arms.

How much she wished now that she had insisted on having time to go to her room and get herself a cardigan to
cover herself with—or even better to change completely.

She knew—just knew from the way Colin's lips were
thinning—what he was thinking.

'Colin. What…what are you doing here?'

The words were out before she could silence them.
Uttering them, she recognized, angry with herself, had
made her sound like an immature schoolgirl, caught out
in some forbidden activity.

'It's all right, Annie.'

How soft and reassuring Colin's voice always sounded.
So kind and caring and reasonable. No wonder her mother
had never understood her fear of him.

'No one's going to be angry with you. I'm here to
make sure of that. You know I've always had your best
interests at heart.'

No one was going to be angry with her? But he already
was. She mustn't let him do this to her. She must *not* slip
back to being the fearful creature she had been before
Falcon had rescued her. *Falcon*. If only he had been here…

'I don't understand why you are here,' Annie told him
flatly. She must be strong and firm. She must behave as
though Falcon were standing at her side, guiding and
guarding her.

'I've come to take you home.'

Fire, like a petrol-soaked rag to which someone had just applied a flame, shot up inside her, ravaging and out of control.

But she *must* control it.

'This is my home now. Mine and Ollie's.'

Colin was smiling at her now—the triumphant, gloating smile she remembered so well, and which before he had only shown her in private. Her heart turned over in a sickening lurch of fear when she realised how confident he must feel if he was showing it to her now, in public....

'This is Oliver's home now, yes. But your home is with me, Annie. You know that. It always has been and it always will be.'

'Let's get this over with.' The Prince spoke for the first time. His English was good but his voice was shaky and unsteady. 'Where are the papers?' he demanded turning to the third man, who had not spoken as yet. 'She must sign them, and then he can take her away. He must take her away before she hurts my grandson. Bring the child to me.'

Hurt Ollie? What was the Prince saying? What was going on?

As the third man came towards her Annie snatched Ollie up out of his buggy, holding him tightly. As though her fear had communicated itself to him, Ollie suddenly started to cry.

'See,' Falcon's father announced fiercely. 'Her brother is right. She is not fit to have charge of the boy. He is afraid of her.'

Ollie afraid of her? Colin her brother? What was going on?

Confusion, horror and fear—she felt them all. Instinctively she tried to escape, turning towards the doors through which she had entered the room. But they were closed, with the two manservants standing in front of them.

Her fear increased, pounding through her, filling her and all but drowning out the courage Falcon had given her. *Falcon.* Just thinking his name steadied her, calmed her. Desperately she clung to it, willing herself to be strong and to remember that she was no longer a child in thrall to Colin; there was no need now for her to fear him.

But what about the Prince? He obviously wanted to take Ollie away from her, and Colin would encourage and help him to do that. Colin had never wanted her to have Ollie. She must not be afraid. She must try to be strong.

'It's all right, Annie,' she could hear Colin saying, in his best kind voice. She struggled not to panic. 'Everything's all right. We know how much you love Oliver. But the best place for him is with his grandfather. And the Prince's solicitor will ensure that the courts think that, as well. We all saw the way you held Oliver over the pond earlier, and I've already given testimony as to how you wanted to abort him before his birth. No one blames you for wanting to do that—not after what happened to you. It's perfectly natural that there should be times when…when what happened to you overwhelms you. We're only trying to protect you and Oliver. To protect you from doing something that you would later regret. It's for your own sake and for his. Imagine how you would feel if you were to hurt him.

'Now, if you're sensible and sign these papers that the Prince's solicitor has prepared, giving the Prince guardianship of Ollie, everything will be much easier for you. I'll take you back to England with me and we can forget about all of this….'

'No!'

The denial was ripped from Annie's throat. Fear was crawling all through her. Surely she could only be imagining this? It couldn't possibly be happening? But it was.

'I'm sorry about this.' It wasn't her to whom Colin was apologizing, but the Prince. 'As I've already confirmed to you, the breakdown Annie had after Oliver's birth has left her very mentally and emotionally fragile. Which is why—'

'She should be locked up with other madwomen, where she can't hurt or harm my grandson.'

The Prince turned to his solicitor and said something to him in Italian, glaring at Annie as he did so.

Colin was responsible for what was happening to her. Instinctively Annie knew that. Somehow or other he had managed to put into action the train of events that had brought her here now, to this room and this horrifying situation.

'I'm not signing anything,' she told the three men firmly. 'And I'm not going anywhere. Not until I've spoken to Falcon.'

Whilst the Prince and his solicitor exchanged looks that resulted in the solicitor giving a small shake of his head, Colin took a step towards her.

As though he sensed the danger they were in, Oliver started to cry in earnest.

'Give me my grandson,' the Prince demanded, setting his wheelchair in motion and heading for Annie. 'He is a Leopardi, and there is no court in Sicily that would deny me my right to his guardianship. Especially when they know of the wickedness of his mother—a mother who tried to deny him life.'

'That is not true,' Annie protested.

'Annie, it's no use. I've already told the Prince everything. He knows that you wanted a termination, and that you tried to have Oliver adopted once you knew that Antonio wanted him.'

Annie gasped. 'That's not true.'

'No, it isn't.'

None of them had heard the doors open, but now all four of them turned to look towards them, to where Falcon was standing.

'Falcon!'

Annie could hear the relief in her own voice. She could just imagine the way Colin was looking at her as she half ran and half stumbled across the room, all but flinging herself into Falcon's arms, but she simply didn't care.

'They're trying to take Ollie from me. They're trying to say that I'm a bad mother.'

'The child is a Leopardi,' she could hear the old Prince insisting, 'His place is here with—'

'With me, Father.' Falcon stopped his father in mid-rant. 'And that is exactly where Oliver will be from now on. With me and with his mother—since she has agreed to be my wife and I shall be formally adopting him as my son.'

Falcon's arm was round her, supporting her, tightening in warning as she made a small shocked sound of protest.

'I should warn all three of you that there is no law in this land or any other that will remove from me the right to be the guardian of my stepson, a child of my own blood, and protector of both him and his mother.'

'You can't do this. You can't marry her—a whore who your brother—'

Whilst Annie flinched, Falcon stood firm.

'An innocent virgin whom your son—thankfully only my *half*-brother—abused and defiled, but who, out of the sweetness and goodness she possesses in abundance, has given to this family the sacred trust of a new life—a child that I will never, *ever* allow to be damaged and corrupted in the way that his father was. However, I cannot blame Antonio alone for his shortcomings. He inherited the weakness and the love of vice that eventually destroyed him from his mother. So Oliver will inherit from his mother great courage and true strength of character.'

As he finished speaking Falcon lifted Oliver from Annie's arms, nestling him in the crook of his own arm, from where the baby smiled up at him. The look of love the two of them exchanged made Annie want to weep with gratitude.

Putting his free arm back around her, Falcon guided her towards the buggy and deftly secured Oliver in it, before straightening up to say calmly and evenly to his father, 'I should hate you for all that you have done to hurt and harm those I love over the years, but instead I pity you, Father. For all that you could have had and have thrown away.'

Her ordeal was over and she and Oliver were safe. Safe here in Falcon's apartment. Safe from the Prince and from Colin perhaps, but she was not safe from her own feelings— from her love for Falcon, deeper and burning even more fiercely now, after what he had done to rescue her.

'I'm really grateful to you for what you've done,' she told Falcon emotionally as she sat opposite him on the comfortable U-shaped arrangement of leather sofas. A coffee table on which she had placed her now-empty cup of restorative coffee was between them, whilst Ollie lay fast asleep on the middle sofa.

Falcon inclined his head in acknowledgement of her words. Her voice was still tremulous with the shadow of the fear she had been through. He couldn't trust himself to speak as yet. His anger was still churning savagely inside him, twisting his guts and locking his heart against his father.

'I'm so glad you came back when you did, earlier than you had planned. I was so afraid.'

'I completed the business I'd gone to Florence to do earlier than I expected,' Falcon told Annie brusquely.

It was a lie. He had been sitting in a café in the square next to his apartment when out of nowhere he had been filled, driven by a sudden conviction that he had to be with her. He'd tried to ignore it at first, but it had refused to be ignored and he had been forced to give in to it.

He'd telephoned his second brother Alessandro from the square, demanding and insisting that Alessandro organise a private jet to fly him back to Sicily, then driving as recklessly as though he had been Antonio and not his normal conservative self from the airport to the *castello*, shocking Maria with his unexpected arrival and learning from her not just where Annie was but also about the two men who were with his father.

After he had rescued her, Maria had fussed over Annie, bringing her the coffee he had ordered for her and staying with her behind the safely locked doors of his apartment while he had gone to speak with his father, demanding an explanation of his behaviour and piecing together what had happened.

Now they were on their own, just the three of them in the peace of his apartment. His suit jacket was flung across the back of the sofa, the top button of his shirt was unfastened.

This was how he wanted his life to be, Falcon realised; with Annie and Oliver, in the love he bore them both.

'I have spoken with my father,' he told Annie. 'And I have demanded from him an explanation of his unforgivable behaviour. It seems that your stepbrother and he made contact with one another—and very quickly both of them realised that the other had a purpose that fitted in well with their own. My father wanted to gain control of Oliver's life, and your stepbrother wanted to gain control of *you*.

'I doubt that my father believed for a second that you intended any harm towards Oliver. However, it suited him to pretend that he did—just as it suited your stepbrother to claim that you were mentally unstable and therefore unfit to have control of your child.'

'Colin tried to do that before. That was part of the reason why I tried to hide from him,' Annie told Falcon. 'He threatened to tell Social Services that I wasn't fit to look after Ollie. It wasn't true, but I was afraid that they'd believe him. That's why I moved flats.'

Falcon nodded his head.

He'd already informed Colin that he would be taken to the airport in the morning and put on a flight. He had also told him that he, Falcon, would be taking legal steps to ensure that Colin was forbidden to make any future contact with Annie or Oliver, and that he would never again be allowed to put so much as a foot on Sicilian soil.

He would never tell Annie about the filth and innuendo that her stepbrother had come out with, or the accusations he had made against her: that she was a wanton flirt who enjoyed encouraging men and had done since her early teens, when she had first begun flaunting her body in unsuitable clothes and encouraging boys to take liberties with her; that Antonio had merely been one of a string of men she had led on; that he, Colin, had been asked by her distraught and shamed mother to do everything he could to put a stop to her promiscuous lifestyle. All were accusations Falcon would have known to be untrue even if the intimacy he had shared with her hadn't already proved to him how innocent she was.

'I expect you've told your father that he needn't worry and that you aren't really going to marry me?'

Annie had spent the last hour, whilst she waited for Falcon to come back from seeing his father, picking over and discarding a wide variety of ways in which she could bring up the subject of his statement about marrying her in a way that would let him know immediately that she fully understood his words had simply been a means of protecting her, and that they had not been intended to be taken as a genuine proposition on his part.

'No. I haven't told him that.'

Annie had sworn to herself that she would not look directly at Falcon, no matter what—because she was so afraid that if she did he would see in her eyes how much she loved him. But now she could feel her gaze being pulled towards his as though it was being moved by powerful magnets. Or as though he was somehow compelling her to look at him.

'Well, I dare say he'll find out anyway in time—once we don't. That is to say, when he sees that we aren't...'

Falcon briskly cut across her floundering. 'I haven't told him for the simple reason that I believe it would make very good sense for us to marry.'

Now Annie couldn't have dragged her gaze from his,

no matter what power had been put at her disposal—because she simply had to look at him and go on looking at him, just to make sure she wasn't imagining things.

'You think that we should get married—to one another?' she questioned Falcon feebly.

'Yes. It's the best and simplest way of both protecting you from your stepbrother and securing Oliver's future within your guardianship. Once you are my wife no one, least of all my father, can make any claim to usurp your role in Oliver's life.'

'But one day you will succeed your father. You are his eldest son. You will be Prince and head of the Leopardi family. You can't marry someone like me.'

'I can marry whoever I choose to marry,' Falcon corrected her arrogantly. 'And if you are worrying that some people might choose not to accept you as my wife, let me reassure you they will accept you—or risk losing their relationship with me.'

'I can't let you make such a sacrifice,' Annie protested. 'You should marry someone you love.'

Falcon hesitated. Should he tell her? Should he admit to her that he loved her? No! He had no right to burden her with his feelings—especially when she was still so vulnerable and upset by her confrontation with her stepbrother.

'Doing my duty is more important to me than love,' he lied firmly. 'And it is my duty to protect both you and Oliver. I can think of no better way to fulfil that duty than to marry you. That does not mean that you have to say yes, though.'

He had at the very least to say that—offer her an escape route. He couldn't leave her trapped and forced to accept him with no way out. His honour and the love he felt for her demanded that much.

Not say yes! When she loved him so much? But perhaps for his sake she *should* refuse. He might say that love wasn't important to him, and she might have taken into herself in silence the pain that careless statement had caused her, but what if one day he *did* fall in love? How could she allow him to be trapped in a marriage with her when he loved someone else?

But if she left him where would she go? How would she ever be safe? Colin would hunt her down—she just knew he would. And Ollie—how could she protect her son from her stepbrother's dangerous malice if she was on her own?

'It does seem to be the sensible thing to do,' she agreed.

Falcon felt his heart slam into his ribs in a mixture of relief and longing. Relief because she had said yes, and longing because right now more than anything else he wanted to take her in his arms and tell her how he felt about her—tell her how happy he wanted to make her.

Instead he forced himself to agree coolly, 'It *is* the sensible thing to do.'

He started to stand up, and Annie's gaze slid helplessly to the movement of the muscles in his thighs. Like sand washed clean by the tide, everything she had felt over the last few hours was suddenly swept away, leaving only that now familiar deep inner ache that told her how much she wanted him.

'From now on you and Oliver will live and sleep here, in this apartment. I'll give you a key, so that if for any reason I'm not here and you feel the need to do so you can lock yourselves in. Although you have my word that my father will not attempt a repeat performance of today's events.'

She was going to share Falcon's apartment. Her whole

body quivered in something that was far more sensual than mere relief.

'There is a spare guest suite,' Falcon continued.

A guest suite!

'Does that mean…?' Annie stopped, her face going pink.

'Does it mean what?' Falcon invited.

'If we are to be married, does that mean that we'll be…erm…sleeping together?'

'It is customary for married couples to sleep together,' Falcon told her. 'But if what you are really asking me is if our marriage will include a shared sexual relationship, as well as our shared love for Oliver, then the answer is that I would certainly like it to do so. But that decision must be yours.'

Hers? Well, she knew what she really wanted to say, of course. She loved him, and there was nothing she wanted more than for them to be lovers in every way there was.

She was hesitating—reluctant to give up her freedom of choice to share her life and her body with a man of her own choosing, Falcon recognised grimly. Well, what had he expected? That she would fling herself into his arms now, as she had done earlier, and this time tell him that she loved and wanted him?

'There is no need to make a decision on that right now,' he told her, as casually as he could.

'Has…has Colin left yet?' Annie asked, deliberately changing the subject just in case she burst out with what she was really thinking and feeling and embarrassed them both.

Falcon frowned as he was reminded of an issue that had irritated him.

'No. The first flight I can get him on is not until tomorrow morning. I'm reluctant to allow him the freedom of the island in the meantime, for obvious reasons. Plus there is the matter of my lawyers applying to the courts for an emergency restraining order, to ensure that he is stopped from coming anywhere near you or Oliver ever again. Unfortunately he will have to stay here in the *castello* for now. You need not worry, though. You and Oliver will be safe in here, whilst he will remain in my father's quarters. A fitting extra punishment for both of them, I think, that they should be forced to endure one another's company.'

Falcon wanted to keep Colin here at the *castello* prior to his flight back to the United Kingdom in case Colin went to ground and was then free to hound her and threaten Ollie, Annie knew, so she nodded her head in understanding.

Could he win her love? Falcon wondered. Was it truly fair of him to even try? In marrying her, was he protecting her or imprisoning her just as surely as her stepbrother had done? Was he doing his duty or was he simply greedily and selfishly seizing what he wanted more than anything else?

He looked at Annie, who had leaned across the sofa to check on Oliver. The look of tender maternal love warming her face made his heart turn over in his chest.

He had to put her first.

'It is my view that for Oliver's sake it is necessary that we marry now. However, if our marriage doesn't work out,' he told her curtly, 'or if at some future date one of us were to fall in love, then we can and will be divorced.'

Annie's heart contracted with fiercely sharp pain. Only one of them could fall in love outside their marriage, and it wasn't her. How would she be able to bear it if Falcon did fall in love with someone else? Was he perhaps already regretting his decision to marry her?

'We don't have to get married,' she forced herself to say.

'Yes, we do,' Falcon corrected her. 'Apart from anything else, there is also the chance that we may already have created a child together.'

Annie swallowed hard against the tight knot of guilt blocking her throat. That had been her fault. He had wanted to take precautions but she hadn't let him. Even more guilt-inducing was the knowledge that she was *glad* she had been able to enjoy the precious and wonderful sensation of his body filling her own without any barriers between them, however reckless that intimacy might have been.

'I'm going to go and tell Maria that you're moving into the guest suite here, so that she can get the maids organised.'

Annie nodded her head, but as soon as Falcon reached the door the knowledge that she was going to be left on her own filled her with so much panic that she stood up.

'Could that wait until tomorrow?' she begged. 'I know that you said I could lock myself in here, but… But I don't want to be on my own whilst Colin's still here. He makes me feel so afraid.' She tried to laugh and make a joke about her fear, adding, 'I don't even think I could *sleep* on my own.'

The minute she realised what she had said, her face burned.

'I didn't mean that the way it sounded. I just meant…'

'I know what you meant,' Falcon assured her. 'And there's no need for you to sleep alone. I am perfectly happy to share my bed with you.'

His bed, his body, his life, his heart and his love—everything he had to give, all of it. But of course, he couldn't tell her that. It would only add another burden to those she already had to carry.

CHAPTER ELEVEN

WHY was being in Falcon's bed tonight so very different from last night? Annie wondered miserably, as she lay alone. It was over an hour since Falcon had suggested that she must be tired—only to tell her that he had some work to finish the minute she had agreed that she was, but that she should go ahead and go to bed. In that time she had showered and dried herself and curled up in the large bed, her heart pounding with excitement and love, her body on fire with intoxicated longing and desire, but Falcon had not come to join her.

Now he was in the bathroom, where he had been for what seemed like for ever, and the unwelcome and unwanted thought was creeping over her that Falcon might be delaying coming to bed because he was hoping that she would be asleep when he joined her. After all, she was the one who had asked to sleep with him, not the other way round.

But the last time he had been in bed with her he had wanted her.

Had he? Or had he simply been doing what he had promised and showing her what it was like to be wanted?

He was going to marry her.

To protect her and Ollie and because he thought it was his duty. Not for any other reason.

The joyful anticipation that had filled her began to drain away. Annie turned on her side, to face away from the middle of the bed. If Falcon didn't want her then she wasn't going to embarrass them both by making it look as though she wanted *him*.

Falcon pushed his hand through his damp hair, having wrapped a towel around his hips. He had just spent an hour desperately trying to pretend that he was working when the only place his thoughts were was in his bedroom and in his bed—with Annie. Now he had been forced to endure the supposedly arousal-dousing ritual of a cold shower to ensure that when he got into bed with her he would have no reason to be tempted into waking her up to take her in his arms.

His body was quite obviously not aware of the purpose of a cold shower, since it was showing every evidence of its physical desire for Annie not having abated one iota. As for his emotional desire for her—his love for her seemed to be increasing with every second he spent with her.

Falcon had believed that he had put in place within himself emotional and mental back-up systems for dealing with every situation that life could throw at him. But he had neglected to prepare for anything like this. Love was something that wasn't going to happen for him, he had decided. It was something he could not allow to happen.

Everyone assumed that in due course he would marry and produce an heir, as countless eldest Leopardi sons had done before him. Deep down inside himself, though, Falcon had questioned the whole concept that being the eldest son meant he must marry and provide an heir. He had two brothers, after all. Then there had been the conflicting natures of the kind of traditional marriage entered into by his parents and a modern twenty-first-century marriage. One thing they shared, though, was that neither of them guaranteed a mutual commitment to a shared lifetime of marital happiness.

He had grown to manhood loathing the thought of making a woman as unhappy as his father had made his mother—the result of their traditional dynastic marriage—but neither had he felt able to trust the longevity of a modern marriage. Especially one that would have to endure the pressures that came with his position as head of the Leopardi family, custodian of its present and future good name, as well as the history of its past. Falcon took those responsibilities very seriously.

Without a really strong, enduring love he doubted that it would be possible to give any children of his marriage the inner emotional security and strength his own eldest son would ultimately need if he was not to feel burdened, as Falcon had from a very young age, with the knowledge of what lay ahead of him. It was, he had decided, better—and easier—to stay single.

When his brothers had married for love their happiness had reinforced his private decision. But that had been before Annie had come into his life and he had fallen in love with her.

Even if they had met 'normally', and fallen mutually in love, he would not have wanted to burden her with the life that must be his. Hand in hand with Falcon's strong sense of duty went an equally strong awareness that his life involved making sacrifices. There was no way that he would have wanted the woman he loved to share those sacrifices.

He believed passionately in Annie's right to her personal freedom of choice—in her right to define her own boundaries and live her own life. The actions of those who had deprived her of those rights filled him with contempt, and an almost missionary zeal to counter them.

And yet now *he* was the one who would be taking them from her by marrying her.

What choice did he have? Without his protection she would be at risk from her stepbrother for as long as Colin lived. The only way Falcon could give her his protection was by marrying her.

Marrying her, taking her to his bed as his love, impregnating her with his child, even loving her—surely these were all forms of imprisonment every bit as bad in their way as the behaviour he had so criticised and condemned in her stepbrother, who also claimed to love her? Love could be a terrible prison when it wasn't reciprocated—for both parties, but especially for the one who hadn't asked for it and didn't want it.

So what was he to do? Not marry her and leave Annie and Oliver vulnerable to the machinations of a man who had already made it very clear that, whilst he would go to any lengths to keep Annie in his life, he would equally go to any lengths to remove her child from her life?

Marry her but ensure that the marriage was in name only, so that he was only violating his promise to preserve her right to freedom on one issue?

In his arms she had wanted him; she had responded to him with passion and pleasure.

Because she had never known anyone else. Because he had sprung for her the trap which had been set over her. The sensuality of her response to him was merely the beginning of her journey into her own womanhood, not the end.

She would continue that journey in his arms.

But because their marriage forced her to do so. Not because she wanted to.

Annie felt the bed depress beneath Falcon's weight, and then the cool rush of air as he disturbed the bedclothes. She waited, desperately hoping beyond hope that he would reach for her, or even say something to her—some words of comfort and tenderness that would offer her the solace of knowing that it wasn't *her* he was rejecting but simply their current situation. But instead all she had was the cold pain of an empty silence.

How could she marry him knowing that he was only marrying her out of some misplaced sense of duty and honour? Where was her pride? Her self-respect?

The same moonlight that had silvered Falcon's body so erotically only a few nights ago was streaming in through the windows tonight, but now it was reinforcing her pain in lying here alone and longing for him.

She forced herself to close her eyes, in the hope that she would be able to escape into sleep, but before she could do so Ollie started crying.

He had been grizzly earlier in the day, his right cheek flushed and slightly swollen, indicating that he was cutting a new tooth. Poor baby—no wonder he was crying in pain, Annie thought sympathetically as she slid carefully out of the bed, praying that the sound of Ollie's distress wouldn't wake Falcon.

She hurried into Falcon's dressing room without stopping to pull on her robe. She was wearing one of the nightdresses that had been included with her new clothes, full-length, in fine pleated sheer soft peach-coloured silk, with darker ribbons that cupped her breasts and then tied at the front. The side seams were split almost to her hipbone, and tied with more ribbons at the top of her thigh. Not exactly practical for night-time nursery visits—but then, she admitted ruefully, she hadn't been thinking of its suitability for that purpose when she had put it on so much as of the speed with which Falcon could divest her of it when he pulled at the ribbons.

As the dressing room did not possess a window, a small nightlight had been left glowing, to give some light without disturbing Ollie, and now, as he saw Annie, he stopped crying. His poor little cheek looked very red and sore, and Annie winced as she lifted him out of the travel cot and then sat down in the chair that had been put next to it, with him on her knee.

A quick inspection of his mouth confirmed he was indeed cutting a new tooth. The moment he felt her touch on his raw flesh he clamped his gums together, in an attempt to relieve the pain, the edges of the new tooth sharp on Annie's finger.

'Poor little boy,' she comforted him. She had got some soothing gel and some medicine in his baby bag, but she'd have to put him back in his cot so that she could get them out, and she knew from past experience that the minute she did that he would start roaring in protest. The last thing she wanted was for him to wake Falcon, so she pushed the door closed with her elbow and then put Ollie into the cot, gently shushing him whilst she searched frantically in his bag for the teething gel and the baby pain relief.

Five minutes later she was congratulating herself on having both soothed Ollie and not woken Falcon—and then, as she straightened up from kissing the baby's sleeping face, she caught the side of the slightly unstable butler's tray she'd been using as a worktop, sending an empty glass crashing to the marble floor, where it immediately smashed into zillions of pieces.

By some miracle Ollie didn't wake up, but the combination of her shock and her desire to steady herself had her stepping backwards, in her bare feet, straight onto a piece of broken glass.

She had barely begun to cry out in automatic reaction when the dressing room door was flung open, and the room itself illuminated by the light from the bedroom. Falcon stood in the doorway, instantly taking in what had happened. Unlike her, he was wearing soft leather slip-on footwear, along with a thick bathrobe.

'Don't move,' he told Annie, stepping into the dressing room and then lifting her bodily into his arms to carry her through the bedroom and into the bathroom, ignoring her protests about the damage that would be done to the bedroom carpet by the blood dripping from her cut foot as he did so.

Once they were in the marble bathroom he placed her on the top step of the short flight of limestone stairs that led down to the large shower area, warning her, 'Keep your foot off the floor, in case there's still glass in it.'

'It's nothing—just a small cut,' Annie protested. She felt so guilty about waking him up and causing all this trouble, but Falcon wasn't listening to her. Instead he was crouching on the hard limestone floor with her cut foot resting on his knee whilst he studied it carefully in the bright light.

'I can't see any glass there,' he told her.

'I'm sure there won't be.' Annie tried to remove her foot, but his left hand was cupping her heel, spreading an unwanted and very dangerous heat through her body.

'Maybe not, but I'm not prepared to take any chances that there is.' Very gently Falcon worked his way round the cut and into its centre with his fingertips.

When he had stopped, and Annie had eased out a long, fractured pent-up breath, Falcon mistook the cause of her relief, looked up at her and said, 'Yes, it does seem to be free of glass.'

Thank goodness Falcon didn't realise that it hadn't been the cut on her foot that had caused her anxiety, but her fear of betraying to him just what his touch was doing to her.

'Stay like that and don't put your foot down on the floor. I'm going to get a bowl from the kitchen, so that you can bathe the cut in antiseptic, and then I'll go and clear up the broken glass.'

He was only gone a matter of seconds, returning with a large plastic bowl which he half filled under the basin tap before adding to it some antiseptic liquid from the bathroom cabinet.

'It will sting,' he warned as he placed the bowl on the floor next to her foot. 'But keep it in the bowl until I come back.'

He was right. It did sting, Annie acknowledged, after he had left her to go and clean up the broken glass. But the pain was nothing compared with the pain of loving him.

The stinging sensation had worn off by the time he came back. He checked her foot after she had obediently lifted it from the bowl, and then frowingly pronounced that the cut was glass-free and clean.

'I can do that,' Annie objected, when he removed the bowl and placed a towel on the floor for her to put her foot on.

'You could, but it will be easier if I do it.'

Easier? To have him gently but firmly drying her foot? One hand cupping her heel as he had done before, the sensation of his touch arousing a wild frenzy of inappropriate images and longings? No way. Sitting there, her hands gripping the edge of the step for fear that she might reach out towards him, was one of the hardest things she had ever had to do.

She had to say something. She couldn't bear the thick, tense silence between them any longer.

'I'm sorry I disturbed you.'

Falcon looked up at her. There was an expression in his eyes she couldn't define—a darkness edged with something fierce and proud.

'So am I,' he agreed flatly.

His response to her apology made her recoil. What had she been hoping for? A gallant remark to the effect that he didn't mind?

He was still holding her foot. Apparently a final inspection had to be made of the cut, a dressing applied to it, followed by a plaster. And then, just when she had thought her ordeal was finally over, and had stood up, ready to make the excuse of wanting to check on Ollie—anything other than get into that bed again—Falcon told her brusquely, 'It might be a good idea not to walk on it yet.'

He was going to *carry* her back to bed. Annie didn't think she could endure intimate physical contact with him that was no intimacy at all—or at least not the kind she so desperately wanted. Her heart was thudding as though she'd been running. Her senses were filled with their awareness of him, their longing for him. She'd managed to hang on to her self control this long—surely she could hang on to it for a few more seconds? Held in his arms? Close to his body? Not a chance.

Panic galvanised her.

She backed away from him, uttering a half-choked, 'No!' that had him frowning and flustered her into hurried speech.

'That is—I mean—there's no need to carry me. I have to go and check on Ollie anyway.'

'I've already done it. He's fast asleep.'

There was to be no escape. He was bending towards her. Annie closed her eyes.

Perhaps if she couldn't see him it would be easier for her?

Big mistake. With her eyes closed, and thus denied the sight of him, her other senses were immediately flooded with an increased awareness of how much she loved him.

She loved him and she wanted him, now and for ever, in her life as he was already in her heart, holding her, loving her, sharing with her the wonderful magic of her sensuality that he himself had shown to her.

Annie opened her eyes.

They'd reached the bed, and Falcon was leaning down to place her onto it. Another few seconds and the contact between them would be broken. Another few seconds and the opportunity now facing her would be gone. Was she brave enough to seize it and risk the consequences? Consequences that could easily include rejection?

She could feel the mattress beneath her. Falcon was releasing her. Already it was nearly too late. Another heartbeat and she would miss her chance. He had wanted her; he was marrying her; he would be Ollie's protector and guardian. Why shouldn't he be her lover, as well? Even if he could not and did not love her? She had enough love for both of them.

Annie took a deep breath, inwardly begging for time to smile on her as she reached up to clasp her hands behind Falcon's head and pull him down towards her.

His, 'No!' cracked through the room like a pistol-shot.

Annie could feel him tensing against her, and she could see the darkness in his gaze. Once such a rejection would have had her releasing him immediately and cowering back in humiliated, shocked pain. But Falcon himself had taught her to take pride in her sexuality. He had even advised her to use her sensuality to choose herself a mate. But of course he had not had himself in mind when he had spoken those words to her.

His hands had left her body and his arms had dropped to his sides. He was standing at the end of the bed, held there by her embrace, whilst she kneeled on the bed facing him.

She could feel a wildness racing through her, smashing everything in its way, filling her with a surge of powerful female determination.

The hands she had clasped around his neck stayed there and tightened together. Her heart, her mind and her body were unified in their purpose.

'Yes.' She rejected his denial fiercely.

And then she reached up and placed her lips against his. Just for a second she allowed herself to savour their heart-wrenching familiarity as her own softened and moulded to them.

She could feel him resisting her, mentally and emotionally fighting her, denying her. But, incredibly, his silent hard muscled tension only increased her determination to achieve her goal.

She kissed one corner of his mouth, and then the other, and then lovingly, with great sensual pleasure, she slowly traced the sharp cut of his upper lip with her tongue-tip, and the full curve of its partner.

In the silvered darkness her own accelerated breathing sent her pulses racing, whilst her heart thundered in a wild, passionate tempo. What she was doing thrilled her and shocked her in almost equal measure.

Her tongue-tip stroked the closed line of Falcon's mouth and then probed it.

Falcon groaned and then seized her, kissing her with a passion that drove her back onto the bed, his body following her own and pinning her there, his hands tangling in her hair whilst he held her mouth beneath his own. His kiss was all that she had longed for and more, and she responded to its command with euphoric delight.

His capitulation had been so swift it had been like ice cracking and splintering, taking them both down deep into the darkness of the passion they were now sharing.

Their clothes, her nightdress and his robe, were removed with urgent hands. Falcon's hands were steady and knowing on her nightdress; her own were eager and excited on his robe.

Just the act of inhaling the scent of his skin was enough to send her over the edge and make her mindless with sensual arousal and longing.

This should not be happening, Falcon told himself. But he couldn't stop it. He was helpless in the face of his own love and longing—unable to deny Annie the control she had taken.

Her face was ablaze with joy as she touched him. 'I want you so much.' The words spilled from her as she opened herself to his possession, wanting it with a sharply sweet immediacy that could not be ignored or delayed. Her whole body quivered with delight as she felt Falcon answer her need, and then flamed with heat when he thrust slowly into her, then faster and deeper, taking her to that place where there was only him and their shared need for one another. All she could do was hold on to him and cry out her delight as each powerful thrust of his body took her pleasure higher.

It was over quickly and fiercely, leaving them both breathing heavily.

'That shouldn't have happened.' Falcon's voice was terse.

'I'm glad that it did—because I *wanted* it to happen,' Annie told him defiantly.

Falcon made a small restless movement, pulling away from her. 'That is because sex is a newly discovered pleasure for you. That is all.'

His casual dismissal of what they had just shared pushed her into saying fiercely, 'No, it isn't. What happened wasn't because I'm like some kind of suddenly sex-crazed teenager. It was because I love you and I wanted to show you that love. Because I wanted to create for myself another memory of sharing the intimacy of lovemaking with you to have for the future. I know you don't want my love, Falcon, and...'

Annie took a deep breath. She had come to a very important decision. 'And you don't have to marry me. Because...because what you've shown me and taught me has given me the strength to be the woman you told me I could be. I'm not frightened of Colin any more, and I'm not going to burden you with the responsibility of me or Ollie. Loving someone means wanting the best for them, and wanting their happiness above your own. You've given me freedom from my past. I want to give you freedom to meet someone and fall in love with them....'

'I already have.'

The pain was so intense that after the blow had fallen she thought she was going to pass out from the agony of it.

'You've met someone you've fallen in love with?' Her lips felt slightly numb, unable to form the words properly.

Because they didn't want to do so. Because she didn't want to confront what speaking them meant.

'Yes. And I love her more deeply and passionately than I ever imagined it was possible to love anyone.'

'That makes you even more admirable for offering to marry me.'

It was the truth, after all—even if saying the words nearly choked her.

'Offering to marry you doesn't make me admirable at all, Annie. It makes me selfish and weak, and subject to all the flaws I was so ready to criticise in your stepbrother. What was my offer of marriage other than an attempt to control your life and take away your freedom?'

'You wanted to protect me.'

'I wanted to keep you for myself. I wanted to bind you to me and keep you with me.'

Annie could feel her heart starting to race again.

Falcon had moved closer to her.

'I wanted all the things with you that a man wants with the woman he loves. But I was acquiring them—and you—through dishonesty. I thought myself so noble and dutiful, but the reality is that I was no such thing.'

'You were wonderful,' Annie told him passionately. 'You *are* wonderful. Oh, Falcon, do you mean it? Do you really love me?'

'You are stealing my question to you,' he answered softly, and she could see in his eyes the light and the love that were glowing there. 'But I am the first man—your first man. I don't want you to mistake…'

'Lust for love? Annie supplied for him, shaking her head as she told him, 'I'm twenty-four, Falcon—not sixteen. I could have broken out of my Colin-imposed cage of fear a long time ago if I'd really wanted to. But I didn't want to. Not until I met you. That first time we met in the hotel foyer, the minute you touched me, I knew that something inside me had changed.'

'It was the same for me,' Falcon admitted. He had taken hold of her hand, and his fingers were now entwined lovingly with hers. 'Although I didn't recognise what I felt for you at first as love. Had I done so, I would never…'

'Have become my sexual teacher and healer?' Annie suggested.

'That is what I should say—but I cannot do so since I have no idea if it is true. Where you are concerned I have no control over my feelings.'

'You certainly seemed to be able to control them earlier,' Annie pointed out.

'That wasn't control, it was desperation. I knew that once I touched you I wouldn't be able to stop. You are far too good a pupil—irresistible, in fact.'

He was reaching for her, and Annie happily snuggled closer to him.

'Mmm…' she encouraged him. 'How irresistible, exactly?'

EPILOGUE

'YOU MAY kiss the bride.'

Annie's face was alight with joy and love as Falcon raised the traditional lace veil which was a family heirloom back off her face and kissed her reverently.

The church was filled with Leopardi family and friends, all come to witness and celebrate their marriage—arranged so hastily, Falcon had put it about, because of the precarious state of the old Prince's health.

Annie smiled a secret smile of private happiness. She might not as yet have the same bloomingly pregnant figure as the wives of Falcon's two brothers, but her and Falcon's baby was already growing inside her—had, she was sure, been conceived that very first time they had made love.

'I love you,' Falcon whispered to her.

'I love you too,' she whispered back.

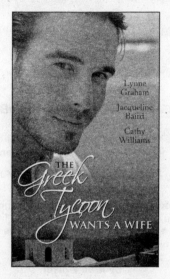

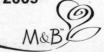

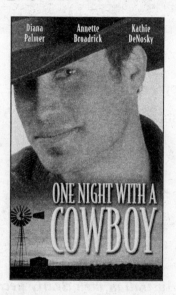

2 FREE BOOKS
AND A SURPRISE GIFT

We would like to take this opportunity to thank you for reading this Mills & Boon® book by offering you the chance to take TWO more specially selected titles from the Modern™ series absolutely FREE! We're also making this offer to introduce you to the benefits of the Mills & Boon® Book Club™—

- **FREE home delivery**
- **FREE gifts and competitions**
- **FREE monthly Newsletter**
- **Exclusive Mills & Boon Book Club offers**
- **Books available before they're in the shops**

Accepting these FREE books and gift places you under no obligation to buy, you may cancel at any time, even after receiving your free books. Simply complete your details below and return the entire page to the address below. You don't even need a stamp!

YES Please send me 2 free Modern books and a surprise gift. I understand that unless you hear from me, I will receive 4 superb new titles every month for just £3.19 each, postage and packing free. I am under no obligation to purchase any books and may cancel my subscription at any time. The free books and gift will be mine to keep in any case.

Ms/Mrs/Miss/Mr_____ initials _____

_____

Surname _____

address _____

_____

_____ postcode _____

Send this whole page to: Mills & Boon Book Club, Free Book Offer, FREEPOST NAT 10298, Richmond, TW9 1BR